SHADOW LAND

HARBINGER P.I. BOOK 5

ADAM J WRIGHT

D1366519

THE HARBINGER P.I. SERIES

I stood in my office, hands in my pockets, forehead resting on the cool glass of the window, looking down at Main Street. It was late morning and the sky was gray, an army of dark clouds marching toward Dearmont from the north. Last night, there had been heavy rain and the streets and buildings still glistened in the pale sunlight. Main Street was awash with rainwater that had formed pools where the storm drains were blocked with trash. Not a great day to re-open Harbinger P.I.

After my trip to Canada and the events that had led to the death of the Lady of the Forest, I'd taken a week's vacation, doing nothing more than staying at home, watching TV, eating junk food, and training in the basement to try and burn off the extra calories.

On a couple of the mornings, I'd told myself I was going to drive into town and open up the office but hadn't managed to actually do it. I'd driven into town one time but had walked past the office and gone straight into Dearmont Donuts, where I'd bought a dozen cream-filled, chocolate-covered pieces of heaven. Then, I'd driven back home and watched old movies with the open donut box on the sofa next to me, its contents disappearing bite by bite.

I'd also spent hours inspecting the sword that hung in a cupboard in my basement.

Excalibur was an exquisitely-crafted weapon, which made sense since it was a legendary sword that had supposedly been wielded by King Arthur. The blade's smooth metal had an unearthly, steely glimmer no matter how poor the surrounding light. The cross-guard was made of gray steel and inscribed with Celtic knot-work that was so fine it could only be seen close-up. The delicate knots formed an infinite pattern of loops, whirls, and curves on the steel.

The pommel was also of gray steel, set with a large ruby that captured the surrounding light in its crimson depths and reflected it in blood-colored flashes.

Red and gold thread covered the grip, giving the sword a regal look. This was a weapon built for a king, a sword sung about by the bards of old, a symbol of righteousness since the Middle Ages, when kings led their armies into battle and knights rode on valiant quests.

And now it was hanging in my basement.

The Lady of the Lake had given me Excalibur so I could avenge the death of her sister, the Lady of the Forest. But all I'd done so far was sit on the sofa, eat chips, and watch TV. There was an evil organization out there somewhere, plotting to destroy society, and I was sitting on my ass watching *Mr. Robot*.

That thought had finally brought me here to the office, despite the miserable weather and the fact that the place felt empty without Felicity. I'd told her to stay in England for as long as she wanted, but I had to admit—if only to myself—that the office felt lifeless without her presence.

Turning my back to the window, I gazed out at the hallway where the door marked ASSISTANT remained closed.

I caught myself sighing wistfully and immediately stopped myself. "Get a grip, Harbinger, she'll be back soon."

It was time to get busy, find a case, do something to occupy my mind. Otherwise, I'd spiral into depression and find myself on the sofa again. I couldn't let myself fall into that trap. There were too many things I needed to look into: the Midnight Cabal, my missing father, and any other cases that might come my way. Cases that would pay the rent.

I realized I hadn't checked the answering machine in Felicity's office. There could be a dozen potential clients waiting for me to call them back about their preternatural problems.

Yeah, right. There'd be maybe one or two potential clients, if I was lucky.

I strode into Felicity's office with a sense of renewed purpose and checked the digital readout on the machine.

Zero.

No messages. No cases. Nada.

I sighed again but this time in frustration. Was there any point in me even being here?

When the phone suddenly rang, the sound cut through the silence like an alarm. I jumped back reflexively and my hip connected with Felicity's desk lamp, knocking it over. It fell off the desk and the bulb smashed, sending a thousand specks of glass skittering across the floor in every direction.

"Shit," I muttered as I picked up the phone.

"Hello?" a woman's voice asked. "Is this Harbinger P.I?"

"Yes, it is," I said, trying to sound light and breezy. "How can I help you?"

"I need you to find my missing child." She sounded upset, her voice almost breaking when she said the last two words.

"You need to call the police," I said. "I'm not that sort of P.I."

"No, I know exactly what sort of P.I. you are, Mr. Harbinger. I'm calling you because my son has been taken. You probably saw it on the TV news. His name is Sammy Martin. He's ten years old."

The news was something I'd avoided the last couple of weeks so I had no idea there was a child missing in Dearmont. But no matter how much I wanted to help, it was a job for the police, not a preternatural investigator.

"I'd like to help, Mrs. Martin, but unless there's some kind of paranormal element to your son's disappearance, I really can't get involved."

"He was taken by a monster," she said matter-of-factly. "Is that paranormal enough for you? Nobody believes me but I saw it with my own eyes. It took Sammy and nobody will believe me. Please, Mr. Harbinger, I need your help."

"Call me Alec," I said. "Give me your address and I'll come over. You can explain everything when I get there." I pulled Felicity's message pad closer and grabbed a pen from the holder where she kept them. Everything was neat and tidy, like Felicity herself.

"It's 34 Smith Street. But before you come over, I was calling to find out about your rate. To be honest, I'm not sure I can afford you."

I wrote the address on the pad, along with the name Sammy Martin. I knew Smith Street. It was in a part of Dearmont where the houses were tired and run-down and the tenants were mostly surviving on welfare. "Don't worry about that," I said. "I'll be there in twenty minutes." I hung up the phone and crunched over the shattered glass as I left Felicity's office.

I could clean it up later. Right now, I had a client to see.

2

When I got to 34 Smith Street, the first thing I noticed was a line of four news trucks parked on the road outside the house. I couldn't see any reporters around at the moment but it looked like the disappearance of Sammy Martin was making headlines farther afield than our sleepy little town. As well as Maine license plates, I saw a "Live Free or Die" New Hampshire plate and one from Vermont, "Green Mountain State."

I parked the Land Rover behind the trucks and walked along the sidewalk to a gate that led to the Martin residence.

The house was like most of the others in this part of town. Clapboard curled away from the walls, probably letting damp inside every time it rained. The paint job had seen better days and was flaking onto the lawn, attempting to escape the decrepit house it had once covered proudly.

Despite the years of decay, though, it looked like the house was being cared for by its current occupants. The lawn was neatly cut and colorful flowers grew in regimented lines along its edge.

Before I could knock on the front door, a woman's voice called out from the other side. "Who is it?"

"Alec Harbinger," I said. "You called me about your son."

The door opened a crack and a dark-haired woman in her forties glanced at me and then at the trucks. She opened the door fully and ushered me inside. "Quickly," she said, "before those vultures get back from their coffee break."

I stepped inside and she closed the door. The interior of the house was as neat as the yard but it was much gloomier in here because the drapes were drawn tightly across the windows.

The lights were on but they threw out a pale, weak glow. There was a strong smell of coffee coming from the kitchen and a weaker, underlying smell of damp coming from the walls. The wallpaper, which looked like it had once been bright yellow, was peeling where it met the baseboard.

I wondered if the dampness that seemed to be creeping through the house was affecting the wiring and making the lights burn more dimly than they would otherwise.

Mrs. Martin noticed me looking at a bulb burning weakly overhead and said, "Those reporters out there all think I'm crazy. Hell, they're probably right. I don't know what I was thinking when I called you. I mean, Sammy can't have been taken by a monster, can he? It isn't possible. It isn't..." Her words faded into quiet sobs. Her legs buckled slightly and she leaned against the wall.

I put a hand gently on her shoulder. "Maybe you should sit down."

She nodded. "Yes, I should do that." She walked unsteadily into the living room, where two weak lamps and a flickering TV barely illuminated a couch and an easy chair. The TV was tuned to a news station, but the volume was turned low.

Dropping heavily onto the couch, Mrs. Martin let out a long sigh. "I'm sorry, Mr. Harbinger, I just feel so helpless. I called you because you're my last resort."

"I usually am," I said. "And it's Alec. Why don't I get you some coffee and then you can tell me what happened to Sammy?" I went into the kitchen where the window blinds were pulled down and the only light came from a desk lamp on top of the fridge. Was Mrs. Martin blocking the windows to stop the reporters peeking in or was something else going on here?

The coffee maker was gurgling, dripping the last of the coffee into the pot. I opened the kitchen cupboards and found some mugs, including a Star Wars mug that I assumed belonged to Sammy. I took out a plain blue mug and poured a drink for Mrs. Martin before returning to the living room.

She took it from me with a nod of thanks and sat with the steaming mug clutched in both hands, her eyes locked on it.

I took the easy chair and asked, "Is there a reason the drapes are closed?"

She looked up from the mug and stared at the curtains as if noticing them for the first time. "I have to keep them closed for Sammy. He has a photosensitive skin condition, he can't stand the light. Daylight gives him hives and a sunburn, even on a cloudy day. He's homeschooled so that means he can't go to school with the other kids. He can only go out at night. He plays in the yard while I watch him from the porch."

Her eyes held a look of sorrow as she turned to face me. "I couldn't even keep my son safe in our own yard. What kind of mother does that make me?"

"Maybe you should tell me exactly what happened on the night your son disappeared," I said.

She swallowed and visibly steeled herself, taking a deep breath before she spoke. "Last night, Sammy wanted to go outside. He hates being stuck in the house all day so as soon as it gets dark, he wants to go outside. I told him to go ahead and play in the back yard where I could see him through the kitchen window while I waited for the coffee pot to fill up. I was going to take a cup outside with me."

Her gaze drifted down to the steaming mug in her hands. "I opened the blinds on the kitchen window and didn't let him out of my sight. There's a little jungle gym out there and he was playing on it in the dark. My sister bought it for him because he doesn't get much exercise. Anyway, I was pouring my coffee and Sammy was swinging on the bars and climbing up and down the jungle gym when he got to the top and suddenly froze, staring into the bushes at the end of the yard. Like he'd heard something there, you know?"

I nodded but didn't say anything, letting her tell the story in her own way, at her own pace.

"I thought maybe there was a wild animal in the bushes," she continued. "There's a stretch of waste ground just beyond the yard, and woods, so it could have been a coyote, or even a bear." She paused for a moment and then said, "But it wasn't either of those. It made a noise, a clicking, snuffling noise."

Again, I said nothing, giving her the space she needed to gather her thoughts.

"It was a monster. It leaped out of the bushes and plucked Sammy from the top of the jungle gym. And as it moved, I could hear that clicking sound, like chattering teeth. I dropped my coffee and ran out the back door, screaming. But by the time I got out there, it had gone. It had taken my boy."

She bit her lip and held back her tears.

"What did you do then?" I asked.

"I chased it through the bushes and onto the waste ground back there. But it was moving too fast. By the time I fought my way through the bushes, it was already in the woods, with Sammy thrown over its shoulder. And he was screaming. My boy was screaming for me to save him. But I couldn't. I couldn't help him."

"What did this monster look like?"

The tears she'd been holding back began to spill from her eyes. She wiped them away with the back of her hand. "You'll probably think I'm crazy. The sheriff didn't believe me and neither did the deputy he brought here. Those people out there from the TV, they don't believe me. Why should you be different?"

"In my line of business, I see a lot of things," I told her. "If I told you about all of them, you'd probably think I was crazy."

She laughed lightly and then shrugged. "Oh, what the hell. What do I have to lose? If it gets my boy back, I'll tell you anything you want to know."

"I just want to know the truth."

"The truth is, Mr. Harbinger, the thing that took Sammy wasn't human. It had gray skin but skin isn't really the right word. It was covered with scales."

"Like a snake?" I asked.

She shook her head. "More like a fish. And it had a fin that ran down its back, also like a fish, I guess. And its face...its face was horrible."

I searched my memory for fish-like creatures from folklore. Mermen, merrows, mermaids, sea nymphs, and selkies came to mind. But none of those creatures could have abducted Sammy Martin because they were bound to the sea, if they even existed at all.

The closest body of water to here was Dearmont Lake and that was freshwater. I tried to recall the lake creatures I'd heard about. Kelpies and naiads were the only ones I could remember. If Felicity were here, she'd probably be able to list off every lake creature ever documented.

I'd never actually encountered any of these creatures nor did I know of any other P.I. who had because the aquatic races were notoriously elusive. They usually shunned contact with humans.

So why had one of them come inland to steal Sammy Martin from his back yard?

"You don't believe me, do you?" Mrs. Martin asked.

"I do," I said. "I was just trying to figure out what type of creature it could be. You said it ran into the woods. Is there a body of water there? A stream or a pond? Maybe something that leads to the lake?"

"I don't know, I never go back there. The police

have searched the area. If there was...anything to find...they'd have found it by now."

She'd thought I'd meant Sammy's body might be there. I decided to take a look for myself before I upset Mrs. Martin further. I got out of the easy chair and said, "Can I take a look at the back yard?"

She nodded. "Yes, of course. I'll take you out there." She put her coffee down and got to her feet. She led me to the kitchen and opened the door that led out to the yard.

I followed her outside, squinting as my eyes adjusted to the brightness of the day after being inside the gloomy house. The jungle gym sat in the center of the lawn, a dome constructed of metal bars that stood maybe seven feet high at its apex. Mrs. Martin had said the creature had plucked Sammy from the top, so the thing must have been tall.

I climbed up and inspected the top of the dome, where Sammy had been sitting, to look for any clues such as a fish scale or a trace of slime but there was nothing there. Last night's heavy rain had washed the bars and left them dripping wet.

"Was it raining when Sammy was out here?" I asked as I jumped down to the ground.

"Only very lightly. When he wanted to go outside, I wasn't going to let him at first because it had just started raining and I could see that it was going to come down heavier later. But he was so desperate to get some fresh air, I told him that if he put on his jacket, he could go out into the yard." Her hand went to her mouth and she seemed to crumple slightly, reaching out to the jungle gym for support. "If only I'd kept him inside, none of this would have happened."

"It isn't your fault," I told her. "Something took him. You can't blame yourself for that."

"Will you find him for me?" she asked, wiping at her tears. "The police are doing what they can but they're looking for a *person*. It wasn't a person that took Sammy."

"I'll do what I can," I said.

"I can't afford to pay you much."

"Don't worry about that." I'd already decided to charge the case to the Society. Although I hadn't found any evidence of the paranormal, I had no reason to doubt Mrs. Martin's account of last night's events. There seemed to be some sort of preternatural creature involved in Sammy's disappearance, so the Society could foot the bill. I'd make much less than if I were working for a private client but my only concern right now was Sammy Martin, not how much I was getting paid to find him.

I checked the wet lawn for footprints, or whatever type of prints a fish creature might leave, but found nothing. "Can you show me where the creature took Sammy into the woods?" I asked.

Mrs. Martin pointed to a line of bushes at the end of the lawn. They were at least a foot taller than me and provided privacy from the woods beyond. I could see an area where a number of branches were broken. "It's this way," Mrs. Martin said, pushing her way through the bushes.

I followed, my shirt snagging on the grasping branches. When I finally reached the other side, I was standing on a stretch of dead ground that ran along the rear of the houses. It formed a twenty-foot wide boundary between the properties and the woods. Because of last night's rain, pools of water had spread over the ground, reflecting the dark clouds in the sky, and the earth had been churned into mud.

"Does anyone come back here?" I asked Mrs. Martin.

"Oh, sure. Kids are always riding their bikes along here."

"Okay," I said. "And where did you last see the creature?"

"Right there," she said, pointing at the edge of the woods. "It disappeared into the trees with Sammy over its shoulder."

I walked over to the place she'd indicated and peered at the shadows between the trees. If the police had searched the woods, it was unlikely I was going to find anything here. I made a mental note to talk with Deputy Amy Cantrell later and find out if the police search had turned up anything.

"Do you see anything?" Mrs. Martin asked from behind me.

"No," I said, turning to face her. I paused and listened to a sound that had caught my attention. A low, rushing sound that seemed far away. "You hear that?"

She listened and nodded. "It sounds like water."

"Have you heard it before?"

"No, but like I told you, I don't come back here."

Rain began to fall, lightly at first and then heavier, splashing into the puddles and rustling through the trees. I could still hear the rushing water in the distance but it was fainter now, drowned out by these new sounds.

"I'm going to take a look around," I told her. "Maybe you should go back inside. I'll let you know if I find anything."

"Okay," she said. "Thank you for taking this case, Mr. Harbinger. I pray you find Sammy alive and well." The tears began again, mingling with the rain on her cheeks. She turned away and pushed through the bushes to get back onto her property.

I stepped into the woods. The thick foliage kept out the worst of the rain in here. I couldn't see any clear tracks on the ground but there were places where the undergrowth had been disturbed and sticks had been snapped. Those disturbances could have been made by a large animal but Mrs. Martin's account of last night's events meant they were more likely to have been made by the fish creature that had abducted Sammy.

I followed the trail to a circular metal grate set in the ground. The rushing sound was louder now, coming up through the grate. I looked at the trees around me. The middle of the woods seemed like a strange place to build a storm drain.

Digging in my jeans pocket, I found the small Maglite I always carried and clicked it on before shining it through the gaps in the grate. There was water down there, flowing along the underground pipe, carrying dead leaves and twigs along with it, but I couldn't see anything else.

The pipe probably took rainwater down to the lake. The creature could have used it to move unseen to and from this area. I inspected the grate. It was clean of dead leaves and sticks, which could mean it had been moved recently.

Taking my phone out of my pocket, I called Amy Cantrell at the station. Her father, the sheriff, was probably in charge of this case but Amy would know what was going on. Besides, I got along much better with her than I did with her dad.

She answered immediately. "Deputy Cantrell." Her voice was clipped, officious, and I wondered how many calls from the media she'd had to deal with lately. A missing young boy was big news.

"Hey, it's Alec," I said.

Her voice was flat, unreadable. "Hey, how's it going? Your office has been closed for a while, I thought you'd gone away."

Thought or wished? I wondered. Even though I'd solved the case of her mother's murder and protected the town from a dark god that had been summoned to Earth to eat everyone, the police still hated me.

Sheriff Cantrell thought I was a blight on the town and had no problem expressing that point of view. I had thought for a while that Amy's opinion of me was different than her father's but since the events at the lake involving the aforementioned dark god, she'd turned cold.

"No, I'm still here," I said. "I'm just calling to ask you something real quick. When your officers searched the woods behind Smith Street, the area where Sammy Martin disappeared, did they investigate the storm drain?"

"What? Why are you asking that?"

"Just wondering," I said.

"Harbinger, what are you up to? Leave that case alone, it's police business."

"Did you hear Mrs. Martin's description of the abductor?"

She sighed. "Yes, I heard it. She said her son was taken by a monster. But wouldn't anyone whose child had been abducted say that?"

"She meant it literally. Scales, fins, the whole monster thing."

"It was dark, it was raining. She was in shock. Just because she thought she saw a monster doesn't mean she did."

"I don't know how you can say that," I said. "After what you saw at the lake."

Amy sighed again. "I saw some weird shit, I can't deny that. But that doesn't mean I can blame monsters for every crime that is committed in Dearmont."

"Only the ones where monsters are actually to blame," I said.

"Harbinger, why have you been speaking with Sammy Martin's mother? And why are you asking me about a storm drain?"

That was the second time she'd called me Harbinger? Were we on last-name terms now? Not too long ago, she'd called me Alec and we'd been friends. At least I thought we'd been friends.

I looked down at the grate by my feet. I had more urgent business than wondering about my friendship status with the deputy. "Did your officers search the drain last night?" I asked her.

There was a pause and then she said, "The rain was too heavy. The drain was flooded. Of course we're going to search it but we can't endanger the lives of our officers."

"Okay, that's all I needed to know," I said. "See ya."

"Harbinger, what are you—"

I ended the call. Nobody had looked for Sammy Martin in the drain. The creature that took him could have used the pipe as a way to get to the lake or could have left the boy's body down there.

Steeling myself in case the latter were true, I hooked my fingers through the cold, wet grate and heaved on it.

The damn thing was heavy and by the time I had lifted it and tossed it into the undergrowth, I was breathing hard, my heart pounding. I was pretty sure that wasn't only due to the heaviness of the grate, though; I felt a growing dread that I was going to find Sammy down there in the dark.

How was I going to tell Mrs. Martin that I'd found her son's body in a storm drain?

Letting out a long breath, I mentally prepared myself to drop into the drain and begin my search. With any luck, I wouldn't be washed away by the raging water and end up floating in Dearmont Lake.

"Alec, wait for me."

I started at the sound of the voice behind me and turned to see Felicity making her way through the wet undergrowth. She was wearing boots, jeans, and a dark red hiking jacket, much better equipped for the weather than I was in my flannel shirt and white tee.

"Felicity," I said. "What are you doing here? I thought you were in England." Despite my shock at seeing her, I was happy she was here. I hadn't seen her since I'd taken Gloria the faerie queen's remains to their final resting place.

"I flew back yesterday evening," she said. "I was going to surprise you at the office this morning but when I got there, you'd already left. After cleaning up the mess you'd made, I came to the address you'd written on the notepad. Mrs. Martin wasn't going to let me in at first because she thought I was a journalist but after I convinced her I wasn't, she told me you were out here."

"Well, it's good to see you," I said, drawing her into an awkward hug. Her hair smelled of apple and cinnamon and the feeling of having her in my arms was a good one, despite the fact that we were both rain-soaked.

She gestured to the storm drain. "So, what are we doing?"

"Mrs. Martin believes her son was taken by a monster last night. A fish-like creature. I was snooping around and I found this. The police didn't check it out during their search of the area so I'm going to take a look."

Felicity leaned over the drain and wrinkled her nose slightly. "Is it safe?"

"Probably not. But if Sammy Martin is down there, I have to find him."

"*We* have to find him," she corrected me.

I grinned. It felt good to have someone on my side, especially after the conversation I'd just had with Deputy Cantrell.

I crouched at the edge of the drain and shone my

light down there again. The water was fast moving, pulled by gravity along the sloping pipe. The question was: how deep was it? I didn't want to drop down there only to get swept away by the torrent.

"We can use those," Felicity said, pointing at a set of rusty iron rungs set into the wall.

I nodded and lowered myself into the hole, searching for the first rung with my boot. When I found it, I gradually put my weight on it. It held. I climbed down gingerly until I was standing in the fast-flowing water, the soles of my boots on the bottom of the pipe. The water came up to my knees and although its pull was strong against my legs, I could stay on my feet with no problem.

Felicity followed me down and, when we were both standing in the fast-flowing water, took her own Maglite out of her pocket and turned it on.

Our flashlight beams illuminated the curved walls and ceiling of the drainpipe. The air smelled damp and moldy down here and there was a chill coming off the rainwater.

"Doesn't this seem like a strange place to put a storm drain?" I asked Felicity. "There's no road or pavement to drain the water away from."

"This is Dawson Street," she said.

"Dawson Street?"

She nodded. "In the early thirties, there was going to be a street here called Dawson Street. The storm drains were put here to serve the road that was going to be built but construction stopped and Dawson Street was never finished."

"Why didn't I know that?"

"Because you didn't research the history of Dearmont like I did," she said matter-of-factly. "Come on, let's see where this leads." She walked forward in the direction of the water's flow, her flashlight beam bouncing off the sides of the pipe.

I caught up with her. "Why didn't they finish Dawson Street? Was the construction crew attacked by something that came out of the drain?"

Felicity shook her head. "No, the explanation is a bit more mundane than that. They ran out of money."

We walked on, trudging through the water and casting our lights over everything, looking for evidence that Sammy Martin had been down here. There was nothing but mold on the walls and leaves and branches in the water.

After ten minutes, we came to another grate. Light filtered down into the pipe from above, along with rainwater dripping off the metal grill.

"We're still in the woods," I said, looking up through the gaps in the metal and seeing branches against the gray sky.

We continued on, leaving the grate behind and becoming enveloped by darkness again, the Maglites providing the only illumination.

Felicity suddenly halted and put a hand on my arm. "Do you hear that?"

"No," I said, "what is it?"

She put a finger to her lips. "Sshhh. There's something in the pipe ahead. It's coming this way."

I listened. Above the rush of the water, I could hear splashes, the sounds of something approaching us from the darkness ahead.

"If it's a clown, I'm out of here," I said.

Up ahead, high-powered flashlight beams cut through the darkness. Now I could hear voices—two disgruntled male voices—complaining about the cold and the wet and the fact that they'd been picked for this "shitty duty."

Two uniformed deputies wearing waders came into view. They pointed their flashlights at us. I recognized them as deputies Elwood and Hobbs.

"Hey, get those lights out of our faces, guys," I said.

"Alec Harbinger," Elwood said, "I should have known we'd find you in the sewer."

"Very funny," I said. "Have you found anything relating to the kid's disappearance yet?"

"We just got here," Hobbs said. "So, no. And even if we did find something, we wouldn't tell you about it."

"Unless it's a werewolf's claw," Elwood said, chuckling. "We'd tell you if we found a werewolf's claw. Or a vampire's fang. Yeah, we'd tell you about that." He laughed to himself.

"You need to work on those wisecracks, Elwood," I said.

He stopped laughing and said, "Shut up, Harbinger."

"Where did you two get into the pipe?" Hobbs asked me.

"In the woods behind Sammy Martin's house," I told him. "How about you?"

"At the next grate." He pointed his chin at the darkness behind him. "Did you find anything down here?"

"No," I said. "Nothing."

"I told you this was a waste of time," Elwood said to Hobbs.

"Well there's nothing back that way," I said, pointing back the way Felicity and I had come.

"We'll be the judges of that, Harbinger," Hobbs said. "We were told to check out the storm drain so we're checking out the storm drain. A civilian isn't going to tell us how to do our jobs."

I shrugged. "Okay, knock yourselves out." I moved aside to let them pass.

Hobbs stepped past me without a word. Elwood, snickering, said, "Watch out for the ghosts down here, Harbinger." Then he put his flashlight under his chin and made a *whoooo* sound, which he probably thought sounded like a ghost.

When they were gone, their flashlight beams receding into the distance, I said to Felicity, "Deputy Cantrell probably sent them over here after I spoke with her on the phone."

"Well, they won't find anything in that direction. There's nothing back there."

"Nope, which is why we're going to go this way." I pointed my Maglite in the direction of the water's flow.

"How far are we going to go?" Felicity asked. "All the way to the lake?"

"If we have to. At least then we'll know if Sammy is down here or not."

"I really hope he isn't," she said.

"Yeah, me too." I was holding on to the hope that the creature had kidnapped Sammy, using the storm drain to get away unseen.

The alternative was that the creature had murdered the boy and left his body down here. The force of the water meant that Sammy's body would be washed along the pipe to the lake.

I assumed there was some sort of grate where the pipe terminated, put there to catch debris such as branches and trash that got into the drain. I was hoping we wouldn't find Sammy's lifeless body trapped against that grate.

After a couple of minutes, we came to the place where Elwood and Hobbs had entered the pipe. I looked up through the hole at the sky above. The rain was coming down even harder now. I could hear thunder rumbling in the distance. Water was pouring into the drain through the circular hole, splashing over the metal rungs on the wall.

"Looks like a storm," I said to Felicity.

"Well, that explains why the water level is rising."

I looked down. The water, which had been up to my knees when I'd entered the pipe, was now a couple of inches above them. The rise had been so gradual that I hadn't noticed it until Felicity pointed it out.

"That's just great," I said. "We need to hurry."

She nodded and we resumed our trek, the rising water splashing around our legs.

"I forgot to ask," I said as we increased our pace, "how is your dad?" Felicity had been in England because her father had suffered a heart attack and Felicity had flown over there to help her mother care for him.

"He's on the road to recovery. The doctor is pleased with his progress and he seems much fitter again. I asked him if he wanted me to stay longer but he said he'll be fine and that I should get back to work."

"That's good," I said. "I'm glad everything is okay."

"Yes, it's a relief. And while I was there, I used his records of ancient Egypt to find out more about

Rekhmire's Curse. There's a way to beat it, Alec. If Mallory puts the heart from the Box of Midnight back into Tia's mummy where it belongs, the curse will be lifted."

"Well, we have the heart," I said. "Maybe we can find out where the mummy is, if it still exists."

"It has to exist for the curse to be active. The legend says that Rekhmire hid the mummy somewhere where no one would find it."

"We're going to have a problem finding Mallory too. I've tried to contact her almost every day since she left but she isn't answering her phone and she hasn't called me back. The last time I spoke with her was when Mister Scary slaughtered all those kids at Oak House." I didn't mention the nightmare I'd had in which Mallory had been trapped inside a mirror.

"I'm sure she'll contact you eventually," Felicity said.

"Yeah, I hope so. Right now, though, we need to find Sammy Martin and something tells me he wasn't taken to the lake. Not along this pipe, anyway."

I pointed my light directly in front of us to where a grate blocked our way. Branches and leaves had collected against the grill, held in place by the force of the water. The grate looked heavy and rusty and was bolted into place. There was no way anyone or anything had gotten past it last night.

"So if it didn't go this way," Felicity said, "it must

have gone up to the surface, probably at that last grate we passed."

I nodded and we retraced our steps. Walking back along the pipe, against the rising water's current, was much more difficult that going with the flow. By the time we got to the rungs, the water was splashing against my upper thighs. It was rising quickly thanks to the storm.

"You want to go first?" I asked Felicity.

She nodded and climbed up, pressing her shoulders against the grate and pushing it out of the way. When her feet disappeared over the edge of the hole, I followed her to the surface and found that we were still in the woods. Thunder rumbled overhead and the rain was pouring down through the trees, streaming off the leaves and branches.

Felicity pulled up the hood on her jacket and began to inspect the area around the hole from which we'd just emerged. "It looks like the creature came this way," she said. "There are broken twigs and disturbances in the undergrowth."

She surveyed the area some more and then pointed down a slope. "It went down there."

"Let's go," I said.

The slope led down to a stream that cut through the woods. The storm had swelled the stream so much that it had burst its banks. It coursed through the woods, sweeping away mud, branches, and leaves as it went.

"I don't think the police have been here," Felicity said. "There are indicators that something came out of the stream and moved through the undergrowth to the storm drain and then later went from the drain to the lake but there aren't any signs of the police searching the area."

"Figures," I said. "They didn't even search the storm drain until I called them."

"Shall we follow the stream to the lake?" she asked.

I shook my head. "I have a better idea, one that means we won't be fumbling around looking for tracks in the mud. We'll be able to see exactly where the creature took Sammy."

"How will we do that?"

"We'll use faerie stones," I said, looking at the tall pines and beeches overhanging the stream. "The trees will show us what happened here last night."

Felicity nodded. "All right. What equipment do we need?"

"I need to mix a couple of potions to make us receptive to the visions and we need the stones. They're at my place."

"Perhaps I should sit with Mrs. Martin while you go and get them," she said. "I'll see if I can get some more information about Sammy. There must be some reason the creature wanted him in particular."

"Sounds good," I said. "The more info we can get, the better. If that thing came upstream from the lake, why not just go to the closest house and kidnap someone? Why leave the stream and head into the drain to get to Sammy's yard?"

"I'll see if I can find out," Felicity said.

We walked through the woods to the dead ground behind the Martins' house and slipped through the bushes into the yard. Mrs. Martin was in the kitchen, looking out of the window. When she saw us, she rushed to the back door and opened it.

"Did you find anything?" she asked, coming out into the rain.

"Not yet," I said, putting a hand on her shoulder. "We're still looking. I need to get some equipment. Felicity is going to stay here with you while I'm gone, if that's okay."

She nodded. "Yes, of course." Then she saw the mold and slime on our clothes. "What happened to your clothes?"

"We searched a storm drain," I said.

Her hand flew to her mouth and her eyes grew wide. "No," she uttered.

"It isn't what you think," I told her. "We were tracking the creature you saw last night. It used the drain to move through the woods, that's all."

Her legs seemed to lose all their strength. She leaned heavily against the kitchen table. Felicity guided her into one of the chairs.

"We didn't find anything down there," Felicity

said. "Like Alec said, we were just following the creature's movements."

Our words did nothing to comfort Mrs. Martin. She put her face in her hands and wept.

Felicity shot me a questioning look. I shrugged. I had no idea why Sammy's mother was reacting so badly to the news that we'd been in a storm drain, especially when we'd assured her that we hadn't found anything down there.

Mrs. Martin looked up at me with eyes that held a deep sorrow. "I don't believe this is happening again. It can't be happening again." She put her face back into her hands.

"Mrs. Martin," Felicity said gently, putting her arm around the distraught woman's shoulders, "what do you mean? What's happening again?"

Mrs. Martin composed herself and looked at Felicity. "Ryan, my husband, was a trucker. He used to haul refrigerators and dishwashers down to Providence and Boston. A couple of years ago, he told me that he felt uneasy every time he had to leave the house because he was sure something was following him. Not some*one*, he always said some*thing*. And he said it was watching from the storm drains. I dismissed what he was telling me because he'd had...problems...all his life and I thought he'd get over it, you know?"

She took a deep breath as if steeling herself for what she was going to say next. "But his paranoia got worse as the days went on. Eventually, he couldn't take it anymore and he got professional help. There's a hospital where the doctors specialize in the kind of problems Ryan was experiencing. He went there for therapy and even checked himself in for a couple of weeks at a time. But then he went missing from there."

The tears came again and she wiped them away. "The doctors called the police and a search was carried out. But all they found were pieces of Ryan's clothing in a storm drain. They'd been ripped to shreds, as if Ryan had been attacked by an animal. His body was never found. And now the same thing has happened to Sammy."

"Listen," I said, crouching down and looking into her eyes. "We didn't find anything at all in the storm drain. I'm going to go to my house and get some equipment while Felicity stays here with you. I promise, we're going to find out exactly where your son is."

I stood and gave Felicity a little wave before leaving the kitchen and going to the front door.

When I opened it, the scene outside was very different from when I'd arrived. There were at least a dozen reporters gathered around the trucks, most of them huddled beneath umbrellas.

Some of them were recording broadcasts, standing on the sidewalk in front of the house with microphones held to their mouths while they spoke to the cameras.

When they saw me emerge from the house, they all stopped what they were doing and flocked to the gate, pointing their microphones and cameras at me.

"Sir, are you with the police?"

"Can you tell us if there is any progress with the case?"

"Could you comment on Joanna Martin's mental health? Is this related to her husband's disappearance two years ago?"

I shoved past them and climbed into the Land Rover. While they were aiming their cameras through the window and shouting questions at me, I pulled onto the street and accelerated, leaving them bewildered in the middle of the road.

I didn't want to end up on the news. The press already thought the monster story was crazy; if they found out I was a preternatural investigator, they'd have a field day. Mrs. Martin had been through enough already without having to deal with that.

I just hoped that the promise I'd made to her in the kitchen was one I could keep.

3

When I got back to my house, I went to the kitchen and found the herbs I'd need for the potions. After grinding them up with a mortar and pestle, I measured them into two glass vials and topped them up with rum.

I put the potions into a backpack and then went upstairs to the spare bedroom where I kept most of my magical items. Grabbing two faerie stones—stones with natural holes in their center—I added them to the backpack along with a couple of enchanted daggers. I wasn't expecting trouble but there was no harm in being prepared for it.

As I left the room and walked to the top of the stairs, I heard something that made me stop dead in my tracks. It also made the hairs on the back of my neck stand up. Had someone just whispered my name? The sound had been barely audible yet I was sure I'd heard it.

I mentally checked the wards around the house. They were still intact, so the whisper had originated from somewhere within the magical barrier.

I took a couple of tentative steps down the stairs before I heard it again.

"Alec."

The voice was cold, faint, and thin and it seemed to be beckoning me.

The scariest thing about it was that I was sure the sound hadn't come from inside the house at all. The cold whisper was rising up from within my own mind.

The air around me felt suddenly icy.

"Alec."

I went downstairs slowly, listening to the house around me even though I was sure the whisper was being transmitted directly into my head.

I walked into the living room and tried to figure out what was happening. The wards were still up so nothing had entered the house, either physically or magically.

The sound was coming from my own mind, which meant either I was hearing voices that weren't there or something was reaching out to me telepathically. Something that was already in the house.

I had a number of powerful artifacts in here but

they were all kept in certain conditions that prevented their power from leaking out. There was only one item that had arrived here recently and was simply hanging in a cupboard without any containment measures holding its power in check.

I went down to the basement and walked across the training area to the cupboard on the wall. The air seemed even colder down here.

I'd opened this cupboard and looked at the sword inside many times but as I reached for the handle now, fear bloomed in my brain like a viper uncoiling itself from a nest.

"It won't hurt you," I told myself as I grabbed the handle and pulled the cupboard door open.

Excalibur wasn't glowing or vibrating, it wasn't wreathed in magical smoke, or emitting glowing eldritch runes. It simply hung on its pegs like a normal sword, giving no indication that it had been whispering at all.

In fact, I was beginning to think I'd imagined the whole thing.

I reached forward and touched the red and gold thread that was wound around the grip. There were no flashes of magic, no voice that suddenly penetrated my mind, just the rough touch of the thread.

After closing the cupboard, I went back upstairs, heading straight out the front door to the Land Rover.

Backing out of the driveway, I told myself to concentrate on Sammy Martin for now. I owed it to him and his mother to put all my time and energy into finding him, not thinking about a creepy legendary sword that was hanging in my basement.

In the rearview mirror, the house receded into the distance but, despite the growing distance between me and it, and despite the fact that the heating in the Land Rover was on full blast, I felt an icy chill creep into my bones.

4

Instead of parking outside the Martin house where the news vans were, I drove around the block and found a place where I could access the strip of dead ground behind the houses.

The Land Rover had no trouble mounting the sidewalk and driving over it and onto the wide area of mud that had once been designated Dawson Street by the town planners.

I stopped at the rear of the Martin residence, got out, and slipped through the bushes to the lawn.

A few moments after I knocked on the back door, Felicity opened it. "Alec, are you all right? You look like you've seen a ghost."

"I'm fine," I said. I hadn't realized until now that the encounter with Excalibur had affected me so much that I was visibly shaken. "Come on, let's go find the boy."

"There's something you need to see first," she said, stepping aside so I could enter the house and get out of the rain. "I asked Mrs. Martin if I could look in Sammy's bedroom. I found something there that pertains to the case."

"Okay," I said, "Show me."

She led me past the living room, where Joanna Martin was sitting on the sofa watching the news on TV, and up the stairs to the second floor. A dim light illuminated several closed doors. Felicity went to one that bore a homemade cardboard sign that read SAMMY'S ROOM printed in green marker.

She opened it and we went inside. Just like the rest of the house, the room felt damp and when Felicity clicked on the light, it gave off a feeble, yellow glow. There was a window that probably looked out over the back lawn but it was obscured at the moment by thick black drapes.

Apart from that, the room was like any other ten-year-old boy's. There was a TV in the corner, a single bed with a Star Wars comforter and pillow case, and a desk with a laptop and textbooks.

Band posters adorned the walls, as well as some of Sammy's own drawings. These were of moonlit forests and deserted streets beneath a starry sky.

I wondered what it was like for this boy, to live in a night world and never see the sun. Vampires lived that way, of course, but they were creatures of the night. Sammy was a normal boy who'd had this

41

nighttime existence forced upon him through no fault of his own.

"Look at this," Felicity said, going to the desk and picking up a black hardbound notebook and handing it to me.

The pages inside were filled with drawings of the fish creature. In some of the pictures, the creature stood on the shore of a lake, rocks and trees in the background along with a full moon in the night sky. In others, it was prowling along a pipe that looked a lot like the storm drain we'd been in earlier.

"What do you think this all means?" she asked.

I shrugged. "I don't know. Obviously, Sammy knew of the creature's existence before it came here." I pointed at a drawing that showed the creature emerging from moonlit water near a rocky shoreline. "Is that Dearmont Lake?"

"I don't recognize it," she said, flipping through the pages of the book and taking a photo of each page with her phone. "It could be Dearmont Lake, I suppose. Or a place Sammy drew from his imagination."

"He didn't imagine the creature that took him last night," I said.

Felicity finished photographing the sketchpad and put it back into the desk drawer.

We went back downstairs. Mrs. Martin was still watching the news in the gloomy living room, her worried face illuminated by the pale glow of the TV screen.

"We're going to continue our investigation," I told her from the doorway. "I'll get back to you soon."

She nodded and said, "Okay," but her attention was on the TV. She was waiting to hear something about her son, maybe that the police had found a body. I hoped I could bring her happier news.

Felicity and I went out back and slipped through the bushes. It was still raining hard and as we walked through the woods, the ground was wet and slippery.

When we reached the grate we had come out of earlier, I opened the backpack and handed Felicity one of the vials. "Here, drink this." I took the other vial and swallowed the contents. The rum burned my throat on the way down and the herbs left an aftertaste in my mouth.

Felicity took a sip and wrinkled her nose. "That tastes terrible."

"Yeah, but it will let us see things we wouldn't be able to otherwise," I said, taking the faerie stones from the backpack and passing one to her. "The trees are going to show us a vision of what happened here last night."

She nodded and waited while I recited the words of the spell. Then she held the faerie stone in front of her eye and looked around. "I can't see anything yet."

"It takes a couple of minutes," I said, bringing my own stone up to my eye and looking at the grate.

After a couple of heartbeats, the image I was looking at through the faerie stone changed. Day became night. It was still raining in the vision but now I was looking at last night's rain, not today's.

"It's working," Felicity said.

The grate was suddenly pushed open violently and the creature emerged into the night. It looked just like the creature Sammy had drawn, with scaly skin, bulbous fish eyes and webbed fingers. Its body was adorned with various shells, tied together with strings of weed. The shells clattered together as the creature moved.

It was carrying Sammy over its shoulder. The boy was crying but he wasn't struggling against the creature's grip, as if he had accepted that he couldn't get away.

"Oh, that poor child!" Felicity said.

When the creature was fully out of the drain and standing on the ground, I guessed its height to be at least seven feet. It would have had no problem plucking Sammy from the top of his jungle gym.

It went over to the grate, picked it up with its free hand, and placed it back over the hole that led down to the drain. Then the creature moved to the stream and began splashing along it.

"Come on," I said to Felicity, "we need to follow it."

We got into the stream and waded behind the creature, following its path from last night. I had to lower the stone every now and then to avoid some obstacle in the water—a fallen branch or a rock—and everything would become bright again with no sign of the creature in front of us. Then, when I raised the stone to my eye again, darkness returned and the fish-thing was there, wading ahead of us with Sammy Martin slung over its shoulder.

Sammy was still crying but his sobs were drowned out by the constant chattering of the shells that hung about the creature's body and collided noisily with each other.

We followed the creature for maybe a mile before the vision vanished.

"What happened?" Felicity asked.

I looked at the woods around us. "We've gone beyond the spell's area of effect. I need to cast it again so the trees here, and the ones farther downstream, show us the vision." I quickly recited the words of the spell and the vision reappeared. We continued following the monster downstream.

An hour later, we reached Dearmont Lake. The woods reached all the way to the lakeshore and the stream flowed into the larger body of water. The creature waded into the lake, holding Sammy tightly over its shoulder. Then it slid into the water face first and disappeared beneath the rain-speckled, moonlit water.

"Alec, it's going to drown him!" Felicity said, splashing into the lake as if she could stop the events that were unfolding before our eyes, even though they had occurred hours ago.

I watched the surface of the moonlit lake through the faerie stone, waiting for the creature to reappear from beneath the surface. Why would it travel from the lake to Sammy's house and then bring the boy all the way back to the lake simply to drown him? It didn't make sense.

"There," Felicity said suddenly. "It's there, Alec!" She was pointing south, at an area where a spur of rock jutted out from the shoreline into the lake.

I turned my attention to that area and gazed through the faerie stone. The creature's head was visible in the moonlight, moving through the water faster than an Olympic swimmer. Sammy's face was also visible above the surface of the water. I could see him gasping and spluttering but he was too far away to be heard.

We sprinted along the edge of the lake, keeping the creature in sight until it swam out into deeper water and then sank beneath the surface again. We waited for it to reappear but its head didn't surface. Only the falling rain broke the stillness of the water.

Felicity said, "Perhaps it went around the rocks and came up on the other side."

That made sense. The spur of rock was at least twenty feet high and if the creature had surfaced on the other side, we wouldn't be able to see it from where we were standing on the shore.

"Come on," I said, "let's take a look." We reached the spur and scrambled up its side, clambering over large boulders until we reached the top. Looking through the faerie stone, I searched the water on the other side of the rocks, desperately hoping to see the creature.

But it was gone. "You see anything?" I asked Felicity.

"No," she said. "Nothing."

"It can't have stayed underwater for long. Even if it can breathe down there, Sammy can't."

"Do you think it...drowned him?" Her voice was hesitant, as if she didn't want to speak the words.

I knew how she felt. The possibility that the creature had snatched Sammy from his back yard and drowned him in the lake was almost too heartbreaking to consider. "No," I said, "it didn't do that. That wouldn't make any sense."

"We have no idea how the creature thinks or what it wanted with Sammy," Felicity said. "For all we know, it might have taken him as food."

I lowered the faerie stone and blinked against the light. Looking around at the rocks, the water, and the rain, I felt frustration building up inside me. We'd seen the exact spot where the creature had disappeared under the water yet we couldn't track it any farther.

It would have had to surface somewhere around here. If it hadn't, then Sammy was dead. I wasn't ready to accept that.

I set the backpack on the rocks and took out one of the enchanted daggers. Its blade glowed bright blue with magical energy. Then I took my phone out of my pocket and placed it into the backpack, along with the Maglite. When I began removing my shirt, Felicity looked at me questioningly.

"Alec, what are you doing?"

"I'm going to take a look down there," I told her, pointing at the water. Tossing my shirt and T-shirt onto the backpack, I said, "Wait here, I won't be long."

Before she had a chance to protest, I made my way down the rocks and jumped into the lake feet first. I gasped as the frigid water rushed over me. Then I took a breath and dived down into the depths.

The dagger's blue glow lit my way as I swam along the edge of the rocks underwater, searching for a fissure or a hole that might lead to a cave. If the creature was keeping Sammy alive, then an underwater cave was the only logical explanation for its sudden disappearance. It would have had to surface to allow Sammy to breathe but it could have done that within a cave, out of sight.

I searched until my lungs began aching for air. When I had to swim back up to the surface to breathe, I wondered how long Sammy Martin had been able to hold his breath after the creature had pulled him under the water.

The moment my face was out of the water, I gasped in a lungful of air. Felicity was standing on the rocks by the water's edge, watching me with a concerned look in her eyes. "Did you find anything?" she asked.

I shook my head. "Not yet. I'm going to try again. There has to be some sort of cave down there, a cave with air. It's the only explanation."

Her dark eyes saddened suddenly. "It isn't the only explanation, Alec."

"I don't believe Sammy's dead," I told her. But even as I said the words, I wondered if I was just trying to convince myself. Felicity was right. We had to prepare ourselves for the worst outcome, but I couldn't imagine having to tell Mrs. Martin that her son was dead. It would destroy her.

I angled my body so that I was facing the rocks and took a quick breath before diving underwater. A swift kick of my legs propelled me down into the cold depths of the lake.

Using the dagger's blue glow to light my way, I explored the rocks again, this time heading out into deeper water. The deeper I went, the murkier and colder the water became.

I noticed a gap in the rocks and swam toward it, dagger held out in front of my face, illuminating the area in a ghostly blue hue. The hole was large enough for the creature to swim through and led deeper into the spur of rock. I poked the dagger into the hole but the glow only penetrated so far. Beyond the blue light, darkness reigned.

Estimating that I had enough air in my lungs to swim a little way into the sunken hole, I kicked forward, feeling suddenly claustrophobic as solid rock seemed to press in on me from all sides. I could only see a few feet in front of my face thanks to the dagger's light and I expected to see the creature come rushing at me from the darkness, eyes flaring and teeth bared.

My lungs began to ache but I pushed on as the tunnel angled sharply upward. If there was a cave within the rock spur, as I hoped, then it couldn't be much farther.

A few seconds later, I broke the surface of the water and took in a lungful of air that tasted of rotten fish. The dagger's blue glow picked out walls of rock that curved away into darkness. I was inside a cave that could only be reached by the underwater tunnel. The fish stench was almost overwhelming.

The question was: who was in here with me? Was the creature lying in wait in the shadows? Was Sammy Martin in here somewhere, waiting to be rescued from the jaws of the monster?

I pulled myself out of the water and crouched on the cave floor, listening for a sound that might give away the creature's location. Something rustled in the darkness.

Staying low just in case the creature came leaping out at me, I moved forward, the dagger held at arm's length in front of me.

The blue glow illuminated the source of the sound, and when I saw what it was, I rushed forward.

Sammy Martin lay on his side on the cave floor, knees drawn up to his chest. He wore a blue padded jacket but it was wet and probably provided no warmth at all. The boy was shivering and the rustling sound I'd heard was his coat moving against the rocky floor.

"Sammy," I said, holding the dagger high up so that it lit my face and he could see me clearly. "My name's Alec. I'm here to help you. Your mother sent me."

He looked at me with dull eyes. "Will you take me home?"

"Yes, I'm going to take you home. Come on, buddy, let's get out of here."

He sat up slowly. His lips were blue, his face gray. "Hey, I know you. You're the P.I. guy. I've seen you around town. You fight monsters."

"Yeah, that's me," I said. "Listen, we're going to have to swim out of here, okay? All I need you to do is take a deep breath and I'll do the rest. Can you do that?"

Sammy nodded. "Okay."

I led him to the water and climbed in, holding my arms out. He slid into the cold water and grabbed me, teeth chattering. "It's...cold."

"I know. Don't worry, you'll be warm and dry soon. You just take a deep breath and I'll get us out of here as quickly as I can."

He took a deep, loud breath and I slid underwater, holding him tightly as I followed the tunnel out of the rock spur and back to the lake. As soon as we were clear of the rocks, I kicked my legs hard and propelled us upward.

We both gasped for air as we surfaced, then Sammy screwed up his eyes and gasped again, this time in pain. "The sun," he said. "It hurts."

"Felicity, get my shirt," I shouted.

She scrambled up the rocks to where I'd left my shirt on the backpack and had returned by the time Sammy and I had climbed out of the water. I placed the wet shirt over his head, protecting him from the sun.

"You okay, Sammy?" I asked him.

He nodded beneath the wet flannel and hunkered down with his arms folded, trying to retain the little body heat he had left.

"Call Mrs. Martin," I said to Felicity. "Tell her we've found her son."

5

An hour later, I was at home, standing in the shower while hot water pricked at my skin, taking the chill from my muscles and bones.

After finding Sammy, Felicity and I had carried him to the highway near the lake to await his mother's arrival. She had appeared two minutes later, driving an old Ford LTD and skidding to a stop when she saw us. I told her it might be best to take Sammy to the hospital but she said she was going to take him home and warm him up with some soup.

She was in such a hurry that she sped off as soon as her son was in the passenger seat, leaving Felicity and me on the highway. We had to walk back through the woods to get our cars.

There were still unanswered questions regarding Sammy Martin's abduction. Where was the monster now? Why had it left him in a cave and then vanished? And the most perplexing question of all: how had Sammy drawn a picture of the creature before it had taken him?

Maybe it had been in the yard before, skulking in the bushes, and Sammy had seen it from his bedroom window. But if he'd seen a monster in the yard, surely he would have told his mother. Why had he stayed quiet about it?

A knock at the door brought me out of my thoughts. At first, I thought it might be Felicity but the knocking was too loud, too insistent.

Grabbing a towel and wrapping it around my waist, I yelled, "Yeah, I'm coming," walked through the kitchen to the front door, and opened it.

Sheriff Cantrell was standing outside, in the rain, looking like a bear that had eaten a lemon. When he saw me, he screwed his face up even further in disgust.

"Harbinger, what the hell do you think you're doing?"

"Well, I was taking a shower until you interrupted me," I said.

"I'm not talking about that. I mean what the hell are you doing sticking your nose into police business where it doesn't belong?" He looked down at my towel. "For Pete's sake, get some clothes on before I charge you with indecency."

I shrugged and went into the living room.

"You're gonna tell me everything that happened,"

he said, stepping inside and closing the front door. "But first, get some damned clothes on. I can't talk to you while you're standing there with all that witchy stuff on your body."

I looked down at the magical protection symbols tattooed on my arms and torso. "You're bothered by these?"

"Just get dressed."

Leaving him in the living room, I went up to the bedroom and put on my jeans and the Miskatonic University T-shirt that Jim Walker had given me a long time ago.

When I went back downstairs, the sheriff was gone. Strange. Why come here to bawl me out and then disappear? I walked through the kitchen to the bathroom door. "Sheriff, you in there?"

No reply. I opened the door and looked inside but the room was empty.

Maybe he'd been called away on police business.

But when I returned to the living room and looked through the window, I could see his patrol car parked next to my Land Rover.

"Sheriff, where are you?" There weren't many places he could be. Unless he'd gone upstairs, which I was sure he hadn't because I would have heard him, he had to be in the yard or in the basement.

Something told me he was in the basement. Maybe he'd heard the same whispering voice that had called me down there earlier.

I went to the basement steps and called down. "Sheriff, you down there?"

No answer.

"Cantrell?" I slowly began to descend the steps. Something didn't feel right. The atmosphere in the house felt suddenly dangerous. My heart began to pound.

When I reached the basement, I saw the sheriff standing with his back toward me. The cupboard on the wall was open and Cantrell was staring at Excalibur. At least I think he was staring at it. His body was motionless, as if he'd been paralyzed.

"Hey, Cantrell," I said, going over to him. "You okay?"

When I saw his face, I took a step back. His eyes, which were fixed on the sword, were glowing blue.

He didn't seem to notice me at all. His glowing eyes stared at the sword and he nodded slightly, as if receiving some sort of secret instruction from the weapon and confirming that he understood.

"Sheriff," I said. Then again, louder. "Sheriff!"

The blue glow vanished from his eyes and he looked at me, confused, as if waking from a deep dream.

"Where am I?" He looked around the basement.

I closed the cupboard, throwing a dark look at the sword. I had no idea what it had done to Cantrell but it probably wasn't anything good.

"Harbinger," he said weakly. "How did I get down here?"

"Come on," I said, taking his arm and leading him to the steps. "You need to sit down. But not here." I glanced at the cupboard. It was probably a good idea to get Cantrell as far away from it as possible.

I helped the sheriff up the steps and guided him to the living room, where he sank heavily onto the sofa. A dazed look remained on his face but at least his eyes weren't glowing.

"Wait here," I told him before going into the kitchen to make coffee.

While I was waiting for the coffee machine to do its job, I called Felicity. She was probably still in the shower or taking a bath because I got her voicemail.

"Hey," I said, "we have a problem. Come over here as soon as you can."

When the machine was done, I poured a strong, black coffee for Cantrell and took it into the living room. I placed the mug on the coffee table in front of him. He stared at it blankly.

"You should probably drink that," I said. "It might help."

He nodded and picked up the mug, taking a sip before setting it down again. "It's hot," he said.

"Do you remember what happened?" I asked him. "Do you know why you went down into the basement?"

He pressed his fingers to his forehead as if that

would help his memory. "I was waiting for you to put on some clothes and then I heard something. Like someone calling my name except I didn't hear it with my ears, it was...in my head. Then the next thing I knew, I was standing in the basement and you were there with me."

"You don't remember anything else?"

He shook his head and took another sip of coffee. "No, nothing at all."

There was a knock at the door and then Felicity came in. She was wearing dry clothes—jeans and a dark blue sweater—but her still-damp hair clung to her neck and shoulders.

"I came as soon as I got your message," she said. "What's the matter?"

Leaving Cantrell on the sofa with his coffee, I took Felicity into the kitchen and, keeping my voice low, said, "Something weird has happened to Cantrell. I left him alone for a couple of minutes and then I found him in the basement, in some sort of trance, staring at Excalibur. And his eyes were glowing."

She frowned and looked past me to where the sheriff was sitting in the living room. "Does he remember what happened?"

"No, he just remembers hearing a voice in his head."

Felicity thought about that for a couple of seconds and then said, "We have to take him to the

Blackwell sisters. If the sword has cast a spell on him, they'll be able to detect it. They might even know what kind of spell it is."

I nodded. Victoria and Devon Blackwell had discovered that I'd had an enchantment cast on me so having them check out Cantrell seemed like a good idea.

"Perhaps there's something in Arthurian lore about all this. I'll do some research. But first, we've got to get the sheriff checked out by the Blackwell sisters."

"I'm not sure he'll agree to that," I said.

"Hell no, I'm not going to go see those two kooks." Cantrell was standing in the doorway. "I heard what you were saying. Don't you worry about me, I feel fine."

"But we don't have any idea what the sword has done to you," Felicity told him. "It would be safer if—"

"I said I'm fine. No sword has done anything to me, so stop fussing over me. Now, I have to get back to work." He pointed a finger at me. "And you remember what I told you, Harbinger. Keep your nose out of police business. This case has attracted a lot of media attention and the last thing I want is for the papers to say a preternatural investigator is making the Dearmont police look stupid. Do you hear me?"

"Loud and clear, Sheriff," I said.

He narrowed his eyes. "Why do I get the feeling everything I tell you goes in one ear and comes out the other?"

I shrugged. "I have no idea."

Shooting me a disapproving glare, he turned on his heels and headed for the front door. "Remember what I told you. Keep your nose out of where it doesn't belong." He left and slammed door behind him.

"He does realize we saved that boy's life, right?" I asked Felicity.

She sighed. "You know what he's like, Alec. He's never liked you and he hates everything paranormal. What worries me is that we have no idea what Excalibur has done to him. What if he's a danger to others?"

I thought about that. I couldn't exactly follow the sheriff around town to make sure he wasn't dangerous; he'd arrest me as soon as he saw me. Besides, there was no real reason to believe that his experience with Excalibur had done anything more than make him confused. Wasn't the sword supposed to be good? King Arthur had used it to fight the forces of evil, after all.

Still, I'd feel better if someone kept an eye on Cantrell.

"I'll go ahead and call his daughter," I told Felicity. "She should be able to watch him without making him suspicious."

"All right," Felicity said. "And I'll start researching Excalibur." She paused and then looked at me sheepishly. "Could I see it?"

"The sword? Sure." I led her down to the basement and opened the cupboard door. The sword hung on its peg, looking innocent.

"That's it," I said. "It doesn't really look very special."

"It's beautiful," Felicity said, taking a step closer. "The craftsmanship is remarkable. Can I touch it?"

"Sure, go ahead."

She reached out and touched the hilt, running her fingers over the red and gold thread that covered the grip and the Celtic knot-work on the cross-guard. "It's amazing," she whispered.

"It isn't talking to you or anything, is it?"

She smiled. "No."

"Okay, just checking. Maybe its interaction with the sheriff was enough to make it go quiet for a while."

Felicity took her hand away from the sword and looked around the basement. "Do you have the scabbard?"

I shook my head. "The Lady of the Lake just gave me the sword. No scabbard."

"That's a shame. The scabbard is said to protect the user from harm." She frowned for a moment, thinking, and then said, "Of course you don't have it. Morgan Le Fay stole the scabbard from Arthur.

That's why Arthur could be killed by Mordred at the Battle of Camlann."

"Wow, you know your Arthurian legends," I said.

"I used to love reading about the Knights of the Round Table when I was a little girl. My parents gave me a modern English version of *Le Morte d'Arthur* for Christmas when I was seven. I used to pretend I was a queen like Guinevere."

She touched Excalibur again. "And this is King Arthur's sword, the sword I read about when I was a child. Here in your basement."

"Yeah, it's pretty cool," I said.

Felicity raised an eyebrow and looked at me closely. "It sounds like you're not impressed."

I shrugged. "Sure, I think it's great that I have Excalibur in my basement but with the sword comes a lot of responsibility. The Lady of the Lake gave it to me so I could avenge her sister's death. That means taking down the Midnight Cabal. What if I fail? What if—even with this powerful, legendary sword—I can't destroy the cabal?"

Understanding flashed in Felicity's eyes and her voice softened. "Because to destroy the cabal, you might have to kill your own mother?"

"Yeah, maybe. I don't know. When Gloria died, I swore to take down the cabal no matter who its members were. And I still want that; the Midnight Cabal is evil and has been the nemesis of the Society of Shadows since forever."

I let my gaze fall on Excalibur's glimmering blade. "But what if—when the time comes—I don't have the strength to kill my mother? If I falter, the people fighting by my side could be hurt."

"You'd never let anything happen to your friends. I've seen how much you care for them. You'll do the right thing at the right time, I know you will."

I wished I could share her confidence.

She put a hand softly on my shoulder and looked into my eyes. "Please don't worry about the future, Alec."

"I won't," I said. "Anyway, I need to get over to the Martin place and see how Sammy is doing. Maybe he can explain how he had a sketchbook full of drawings of the creature that abducted him. And the damned thing is still on the loose so I'll need to figure out a way to catch it."

"Do you want me to come with you or shall I begin my research into Excalibur?"

I looked at the sword again. "Some research would be good. The sooner we know what we're dealing with, the better."

"All right, I'll get started." She walked across the training area to the basement steps.

"Felicity..." I said.

She turned to face me. "Yes?"

"It's good to have you back. I missed you."

A smile lit her face. "It's good to be back. I missed

you too." She continued up the stairs and then stopped halfway up. "Alec?"

"Yeah?"

"Don't forget to ring Amy Cantrell regarding her father."

"Doing it now," I told her, fishing my phone out of my jeans.

6

Amy Cantrell didn't sound too pleased to hear my voice. In fact, as soon as she answered the call, she sounded pissed. "What do you want, Harbinger?"

I wasn't sure when my relationship with Amy had become derailed. Not too long ago—when I'd been investigating Deirdre Summers' murder—Amy had given me a police file and had said she was glad I was on the case.

When that investigation had led to the discovery that Amy's mother had been killed while helping a preternatural investigator spy on an evil cult, Amy had seemed grateful for the newfound information.

But now, something had driven a wedge between us and I had no idea what it was.

"Listen," I said, "I think you should keep an eye on your dad for a while, see if he starts acting strangely or anything."

There was a pause while she processed this and then she asked, "What the hell are you talking about?"

I closed the cupboard door and ascended the basement steps as I spoke. "He came over here earlier and he...became a little mesmerized by one of the enchanted items in the house. I just think it would be a good idea if you make sure it hasn't affected him too adversely. I'd do it myself but, as you know, your dad and I don't see eye to eye on most things."

She sighed. "You can't really blame him, can you? Since you came to this town, we've had to deal with zombies and God-knows-what that thing at the lake was. He lost more deputies this year than any other year of his career. And let's not forget that he also lost his wife to this supernatural bullshit."

I wanted to tell her I was sorry for all that but I knew she wouldn't listen. She was hurting, and right now, she blamed me for her pain. "If you could just keep an eye—"

"Go to hell." She ended the call.

I put the phone in my pocket and grabbed my car keys. As I went outside and climbed into the Land Rover, I admitted to myself that I envied my friend Jim Walker, who had a close working relationship with the Ontario police.

But I couldn't let my floundering relationship with Dearmont law enforcement get in the way of my job. I had to do what I thought was right and if finding lost children meant stepping on their toes, then so be it.

I drove across town to the Martin residence. When I got there, the news trucks were still parked on the street and the reporters were crowded around the gate, so I kept driving and parked on the dead ground behind the house.

A couple of seconds after I knocked on the back door, Mrs. Martin's voice came from within the house, "Who is it?"

"It's Alec," I said.

She let me in, quickly closing the door behind me. "Mr. Harbinger, I don't know how to thank you for finding my boy. I'm sorry I rushed away earlier, I just needed to get Sammy home. I laundered your shirt for you." She pointed at the kitchen table where my flannel shirt sat, dry and neatly folded.

"Thanks," I said.

"And I called the sheriff and told him that you'd found Sammy. And do you know what he said? He didn't say he was glad that Sammy was safe. Instead, he said, 'Well, Harbinger may have found the kid but did he catch the guy who took him?' I told him it wasn't a 'guy' it was a monster and that you believed me about that. And I said that you'd succeeded where they'd failed and they could all shove it. He wasn't too happy about that."

That probably explained why Cantrell came over to my house to bawl me out. He was pissed at being told to shove it by a woman he'd been trying to help. I couldn't blame him.

"How is Sammy doing?" I asked her. "I was hoping I could speak with him."

"Of course. He's watching TV. Go right in, I'm sure he'll be pleased to see you. Would you like coffee?"

"That'd be great," I said. I went into the darkened living room where Sammy was sitting on the sofa, feet curled beneath him. He was wearing a bulky, dark blue hoodie and jeans and looked much better than the last time I'd seen him. A light gray blanket lay on the sofa next to him.

"Hey, Sammy. Mind if I sit down?"

He turned from the TV to look at me and a smile lit his face. "Hi, Alec. Sure, you can sit right here."

He moved the blanket out of the way and I sat next to him.

"How are you doing?" I asked.

"Okay, I guess. At least I'm not so cold now."

"That's good. Do you remember much about what happened to you?"

"I remember everything. The shellycoat took me to its cave. And then it left me there."

"Shellycoat?"

He nodded and frowned at me as if I should know what he was talking about. "Shellycoat."

I ran the name through my mind. I'd heard it before, maybe in a lecture at the Academy of

Shadows a long time ago. I hadn't paid it much attention at the time, but now, hearing the unusual name brought back a memory of a summer afternoon lecture on Scottish folklore. The shellycoat was a mythical creature that was said to live in the rivers and lochs of Scotland. I was pretty sure the lecturer had said the creature was nothing more than a legend and didn't actually exist.

Obviously, he'd been wrong.

"How do you know it's called a shellycoat?" I asked Sammy.

"My dad knew all about them. He told me stories when I was a little kid."

"Ryan was always talking about them," Mrs. Martin said from the doorway. She was standing there holding two mugs of steaming coffee. "He used to tell Sammy about shellycoats and other creatures. I think his own father used to tell him the same stories when he was a kid, stories about the land of Faerie and the creatures that live there. There was a family legend that Ryan's great-grandfather had seen a shellycoat in a river in Scotland."

"Is that why you drew those pictures in your notebook?" I asked Sammy. "Because your dad told you stories about shellycoats?"

Sammy shook his head. "I didn't draw those, my dad did."

"He was always drawing pictures of it," Mrs. Martin said. "He even made some paintings of it a few years ago. Usually it was just doodles, though. Sammy has treasured the notebook ever since his dad died, against my better judgment because it gives him nightmares sometimes."

"So you knew what the creature was when it took Sammy?"

She gave me one of the mugs. "I didn't recognize it at the time. I was panicking. Seeing a drawing in a notebook is one thing but watching a real monster carry your child away is something else."

"But you realized later that it was the shellycoat?"

She shrugged. "I still wasn't sure. The things Ryan drew were figments of his imagination. He had problems all his life with hallucinations, ever since he was a kid. That's why he had to go to Butterfly Heights for help. And when he was home in between therapy, he seemed to get worse, not better."

"Butterfly Heights?" I asked.

"It's a psychiatric hospital up at Moosehead Lake," she said. "The place where Ryan disappeared."

"Is Moosehead Lake far from here?"

She shook her head. "Not really. It's up in the Highlands, an hour and a half north from here."

"Do you know the name of the doctor who treated Ryan?"

"Yes, it's Dr. Campbell—Dr. Robert Campbell.

You think that what happened to Ryan is connected to what happened to Sammy last night, don't you?"

"It's too coincidental to ignore. The same creature your husband thought was following him turned up in your yard. Ryan went missing while he was at Butterfly Heights, so I think it's a good place to start my investigation."

"Do you want the address? I have it around here somewhere."

"I'll find it," I said to Mrs. Martin. "Thanks."

"Thank *you*," she said. "For helping us, I mean. I don't know what I'd have done without you. Sammy might still be out there, lost and alone." Tears welled in her eyes.

I put a comforting hand on her shoulder. "It's okay, we found him. But I suggest Sammy stays in the house for a while, at least until I catch that creature."

She nodded. "Of course. I don't think he wants to go outside anyway, not after what happened."

"No way," Sammy said. "It's too scary. I'd only go out if Alec was there to protect me."

"Don't worry," I told him. "Once this is sorted out, you'll be able to go outside again." I drank the coffee quickly, reflecting that Sammy and his mother would probably never go out into the night without feeling some degree of fear. They now knew that monsters—real monsters, the stuff of nightmares—existed. That was something that was difficult to forget, especially when the sun sank beyond the horizon and darkness crept over the world.

"Thanks for the coffee," I said, handing the empty mug to Mrs. Martin. "I'll see what I can find out from the doctors at Butterfly Heights and get back to you soon. See you later, Sammy."

He waved, then turned his attention to the TV.

I walked through the house to the kitchen, picked up my freshly-laundered shirt, and went out through the back door, walking hastily across the yard to the bushes because of the rain.

When I got to the Land Rover, I climbed in behind the wheel and used my phone to search for Butterfly Heights. I found an address in Northern Maine and a phone number but nothing else. I'd expected the place to at least have a website with photos and maybe the names of senior staff members but there was nothing like that at all, just the address and phone number listed in a directory of hospitals in the state.

I called Felicity. It took her a while to answer and I assumed she was probably deep in research, barely aware that her phone was ringing. I listened to the rain bouncing off the roof while I waited.

When she finally picked up, I said, "How would you like to go on a road trip?"

"A road trip? Where to?"

"Moosehead Lake, Northern Maine." I told her about Robert Campbell and Butterfly Heights.

"Sounds intriguing," she said. "Will we be staying overnight?"

I hadn't thought about that. "Sure, why not? We don't need to rush back to Dearmont."

"I'll make some arrangements online," she said. "There's bound to be a hotel nearby. And I won't even have to pack my things, they're still in my suitcase."

"Great. Meet me at my place in half an hour."

"All right, I'll see you then." She hung up.

As I started the engine and checked the rearview mirror, I realized there was a smile on my face. It would be good to go on a road trip with Felicity. I really had missed her.

I looked up at the sky, deciding that if the weather improved, I'd take that as a sign that this case would be solved quickly and easily.

But the rain continued to fall, tapping on the Land Rover's roof like a thousand tiny claws.

7

It was still raining an hour and a half later as I drove the Land Rover north along State Route 6 toward Moosehead Lake. In sharp contrast to the gray sky, the landscape was composed of vivid oranges and yellows. The fall foliage gave the illusion that the trees were on fire.

"It's beautiful," Felicity said, watching the scenery roll by her window. "We don't get anything like this in England. Nothing this spectacular."

I nodded in agreement. The view through the windshield was spectacular but my eyes were fixed on the road ahead, my mind mulling over the case. "Did you find a hotel?"

"Yes," she said. "There's a lodge in Greenville called the Lake Shore Lodge. I booked us in there for tonight."

"Great."

"I wonder why the hospital is called Butterfly Heights," Felicity said. "I looked it up online but couldn't find anything. There isn't really any information at all about it. It's a mystery."

"The Mystery of Butterfly Heights," I said. "Sounds like the title of a gothic romance novel."

She grinned. "Perhaps there'll be a tall, dark, handsome stranger there with a tortured past and a passion that is all-consuming."

I raised an eyebrow. "A passion for what?"

"For butterflies, of course."

We laughed. The easiness that existed between us had returned and it felt good.

"Oh, this is the place," she said as we drove past a sign that said *Welcome to Greenville, Gateway to the Moosehead Lake Region*. "This is where the lodge is. Should we go there and get our keys?"

"No, we can do that later. Let's see if we can solve the mystery of Butterfly Heights first." The truth was, I was intrigued to see the mental health facility that had no internet presence.

"Yes, I must admit I am quite curious," Felicity said.

We drove through Greenville and followed Route 6 north along the edge of the lake for twenty minutes until the GPS told me to make a left turn.

After I made the turn, we were on a narrow road that led away from the lake and through the woods. There had been no sign on the main road to indicate this smaller road led anywhere in particular.

Rain continued to pound the Land Rover. The trees sagged over the road, dead orange and yellow leaves so thick on the blacktop that they almost covered it completely.

"Well, this isn't spooky at all," Felicity said.

After twenty minutes, the road ended with no warning. It simply terminated in a roughly-circular clearing. A dozen or so vehicles were parked there.

"Destination reached," the GPS said.

I found a space for the Land Rover and killed the engine.

Felicity grabbed her blue waterproof jacket from the back seat, opened her door and slid out, putting on the jacket and pulling up the hood against the rain. She looked at the cars and the surrounding trees. "Why have a car park in the middle of nowhere?"

I grabbed my own jacket—a black field jacket I'd picked up at an army surplus store—and got out of the Land Rover. "Maybe the place can only be reached by foot." I shrugged the jacket on and pulled up the hood. "Anyway, this is definitely the correct parking lot." I pointed at a small wooden sign that said *Butterfly Heights*. Beyond the sign, a path led into the trees.

Felicity lowered her rain-spattered glasses and looked over the top of them at the path. "Like I said, not spooky at all." Then she pointed over the trees and said, "I think I know why the car park is here and not at the facility itself."

I looked at where she was pointing. Maybe half a mile away, a steep hill rose up out of the woods. And on top of the hill sat a building that must be Butterfly Heights.

We'd joked about it earlier but Butterfly Heights looked as if it had actually sprung from the pages of a gothic novel. A sprawling Victorian building with high gables and arched windows, it sat imposingly atop the hill and I felt that there were many pairs of eyes behind those windows, all looking down on us malevolently.

Only the upper floors could be seen from our vantage point because a high wall surrounded Butterfly Heights, obscuring the lower part of the building and the grounds on which it stood. The path that led through the trees from the parking lot climbed the hill to a tall black iron gate, which was closed.

"Yeah, I think that's the place," I said. I almost expected lightning to shoot from the heavens and illuminate the building with an eerie glow but the sky remained quiet and the only glow came from the lit windows of Butterfly Heights.

Once we were on the path and beneath the sheltering trees, we removed our hoods. Rainwater dripped from branches and rustled through leaves, making the trees seem alive.

"Do you think Dr. Campbell will know anything that can help us?" Felicity asked.

"He should know the details of Ryan's disappearance. Maybe he'll tell us more about Ryan's paranoia. Although, right now, I don't think Ryan was paranoid at all."

"Because he really was being followed by monsters?"

"It seems likely now that the creature he told his son about has turned out to be real."

The path began to climb the hill, gently at first, then at a steeper angle. By the time we reached the large black wrought-iron gate, Felicity and I were breathing heavily. Beyond the gate, we could see the grounds of Butterfly Heights. The lawns probably looked nice in the summer but were covered with dead leaves at the moment.

"This place isn't very welcoming," Felicity said, leaning on the stone wall as she tried to get her breath back.

"We'll probably find out exactly how not-welcoming it is in a minute," I said, pressing the button on an intercom that was set into the wall beside the gate. "Robert Campbell might not want to see us at all."

The intercom crackled and then a male voice

said, "Welcome to Butterfly Heights, how can I help you today?"

"Hi, we're here to see Dr. Robert Campbell."

"Do you have an appointment?"

"No."

"Is Dr. Campbell expecting you?"

"No, as I said, we don't have an appointment."

"And what is the nature of your visit?"

"We want to speak with him regarding a former patient."

"Your name, please?"

"Alec Harbinger. I'm here with my associate, Felicity Lake. Tell Dr. Campbell we've come from Dearmont and our visit concerns Ryan Martin."

"Just a moment, please."

There was silence for a couple of minutes. We stood in the rain and cast doubtful looks at each other. If Robert Campbell didn't want to see us, we'd be heading back down the hill and back to the car in a few minutes.

The intercom crackled again. "Dr. Campbell is with a patient at the moment but he'll see you when he's finished, if you don't mind waiting."

"We don't mind at all," I said.

A buzzer sounded and the gate began to swing open. "Please come directly to the door marked *Reception*," the voice said.

We walked through the gate and followed a

gravel pathway that bisected the huge, leaf-strewn lawn and led to the building.

The gate swung shut behind us and the lock clicked into place.

Now that we were within the grounds, I could see that the building had four levels. It was a big place, sitting out here in the middle of nowhere. And the entire building seemed to be the original Victorian-era structure.

In fact, the only modern thing about Butterfly Heights was the security system, which consisted of the electronic gate and a dozen cameras bolted onto the house and the walls. As we approached a large weathered wooden door that bore a small plaque reading *Reception*, I noticed the camera closest to us swivel slightly to follow our progress. Above the door, the year *1894* had been engraved on one of the bricks.

There was a click and the door opened before we reached it. For some reason, the opening line of an old children's poem crept into my head.

"Will you walk into my parlor?" said the spider to the fly.

8

We stepped through the doorway and into a large reception area that was furnished with a half dozen plastic chairs, the magazine-strewn table that was obligatory in all waiting areas, and a hatch in the wall through which could be seen an office. The exterior of the building may have been untouched by time but the interior had been updated.

Sitting at the desk in the office was a man in his thirties dressed in a white shirt with the sleeves rolled up to his elbows and a dark blue tie. He was in the process of getting up out of his chair as I approached the hatch. There was a control panel and five monitors on his desk, showing various views from the cameras outside.

At a second desk, a similar control panel and a bank of monitors showed images from cameras within the building. I could see a room with people sitting at tables, playing card games and chess. Another monitor showed what I assumed to be a group therapy session with a group of people who were sitting in a circle, deep in discussion.

The receptionist, whose name badge simply said Steve, with no last name, smiled thinly and passed me a clipboard with a sheet of paper attached to it. "If you could just sign in, Dr. Campbell will see you shortly." I scanned the form attached to the clipboard and wrote my own and Felicity's names under the *Visitors* section. Under the heading *Company*, I wrote *Harbinger P.I.* Then I signed my name.

Steve no-last-name looked at what I'd written and said, "You're a P.I. Is that private investigator?"

"No, it's preternatural."

He raised a questioning eyebrow. "A preternatural investigator?"

I nodded. "Is that a problem?"

"Does Dr. Campbell know you're a preternatural investigator?"

"Not unless he's psychic."

He hesitated, staring at the words I'd written as if they were going to jump off the page and bite him. Then he put the clipboard away quickly and said, "Please, take a seat."

I went over to the seating area where Felicity was already sitting in one of the plastic chairs and reading a magazine.

"That didn't go well," she said, not looking up from the magazine as I sat beside her.

I peered through the hatch and saw Steve on the phone. I couldn't hear what he was saying but I assumed he was informing Dr. Campbell of my profession. "He doesn't like the fact that I'm a P.I."

"Most people don't," Felicity said. "The sheriff has a bee in his butt about it, his daughter has a problem with you—although I think that's because she secretly fancies you—and those two deputies we met in the storm drain think the whole thing is a joke."

"It comes with the job," I said. "I'm used to it."

"The question is, why does the receptionist think it's such a big deal that a preternatural investigator has come to talk to Dr. Campbell? Is there some preternatural activity here?"

"Maybe they just hate P.I.s like everyone else," I suggested.

"Not everyone hates P.I.s," she said, flashing a smile at me.

A door opened and a tall, dark-haired man dressed in jeans and a dark blue sweater came into the room. He was maybe fifty years old but he looked slim and fit. He looked at me through wire-rimmed glasses and said, "Mr. Harbinger?"

I got up and saw a name badge hanging on a lanyard around his neck. "Dr. Campbell. Thanks for agreeing to see us. This is my associate, Felicity Lake."

"Nice to meet both of you," he said, shaking our hands. His grip was strong and firm. I gave him my card and he put it into his back pocket. "Come with me to my office and we can talk."

He led us through the door and along a corridor to a door that bore his name. He opened it and gestured us inside. "Please, after you. Take a seat."

The office was dimly-lit by weak daylight creeping in through an arched window high above a large desk. Campbell turned on a floor lamp near the desk but it did little to illuminate the room and gave off a pale, sickly glow.

The only other furnishings in the room were two wooden-framed, upholstered chairs on this side of the desk and a large leather chair on the other. A computer sat on the desk but other than that, the room was empty. I got the feeling Dr. Campbell didn't spend a lot of time in here. Or maybe this wasn't his main office, despite his name being on the door.

Felicity and I sat in the pair of chairs and Campbell went to the opposite side of the desk. But instead of sitting in the leather chair, he remained standing. This was psychology 101; seat your guests and remain standing yourself so you appear more dominant, more in control of the meeting.

"What can I do for you?" he asked. "Our receptionist tells me you're here to talk about Ryan Martin. Has he been found? Or—God forbid—did they find his body?"

"We're here to ask you some questions about Ryan," I told him.

He looked confused for a moment. "I thought you were here because you knew something about his disappearance. I don't see how I can help you. I told the police everything I know two years ago."

"We're looking at the case from a different perspective," I said.

A look of understanding settled in his face. He pointed at me and smiled. "Ah, I see what you're doing. You're a preternatural investigator, so you're wondering if Ryan Martin was actually killed by the monsters he believed were following him. I can assure you, he was not."

"So what do you think happened?" I asked him.

"What happened is really quite simple, Mr. Harbinger. Ryan left the hospital one night and went down to the main road. When he got there, he entered a storm drain, probably to face the monster he imagined was following him. He got lost in the tunnels and perished. The police were satisfied with that explanation."

"You said Ryan left the hospital but how did he do that? You have a tight security system here. Locks on the gate, cameras everywhere. How could he escape into the night without being seen?"

He looked a little uncomfortable for the first time since we'd come in here. "The cameras saw him but by the time we had a chance to react, he was gone. He climbed over the gate like a monkey and by the time security got out there, Ryan was already gone, running down the trail to the road."

"Sounds like he was determined to get out of here."

"He was obviously experiencing a psychotic break. He probably thought everyone in the hospital was after him and he had to get away. He often suffered from extreme paranoia."

"And then he climbed into a storm drain."

"Yes, our security team followed him down to the road and saw him entering the drain. One of them followed Ryan into the drain but all he found were shreds of clothing. The police later found more clothing, deeper inside the tunnel."

"So it looks like Ryan was attacked down there," I said.

Campbell sighed. "No, it does not. Mr. Harbinger, all of our patients here at Butterfly Heights suffer from delusions similar to the ones Ryan Martin experienced. Patients with paranoid fantasies are our specialty and we know how they behave. Ryan believed there were monsters living in the sewers. So for him to have a violent episode inside a sewer and tear off his own clothing is not unusual. Not unusual at all."

"You specialize in cases like Ryan's?"

"Yes, all of our patients suffer from paranoid delusions. They come here from all over the country, most of them sent here from other institutions, because we have the best medical team to deal with such people."

I wondered how many of the people here had been diagnosed with a mental illness when actually they had encountered the preternatural world and not recognized it as real, believing instead that they were losing their minds.

"I can give you the tour, if you like," Campbell said. "Then your visit won't have been totally in vain."

The subtext of what he was saying was that this interview was over. "Sure, I'd like to look around," I said. "How about you, Felicity?"

"Yes," she said, "definitely. And, Dr. Campbell, perhaps you could tell us where the name Butterfly Heights came from."

"I can do better than that," he said, suddenly cheery. "I can show you. Come with me. Then you can be on your way. I'm sure you have more important business to attend to than this wild goose chase." He stopped and turned to me. "Mr.

Harbinger, I'm guessing you were hired to pursue this case by Ryan's wife Joanna. Correct?"

"I'm afraid I can't discuss that, it's confidential."

"Well, there's no need to tell me. Who else would have hired you to follow this dead end? I suppose she didn't mention that she was a patient here." He resumed walking.

I said nothing.

"This is where she and Ryan met," he said, opening a door with a keycard. "Joanna came here for therapy because she was having vivid nightmares every night of creatures chasing her through a shadowy world. After she attended therapy here and was prescribed medication, the nightmares went away."

A look of concern flashed in his eyes and I couldn't tell if it was real or fake. "But I believe she may now be experiencing a relapse. That is why she thinks her son was kidnapped by a monster. Yes, I saw the report on the news this morning. You were on there too, although you seemed to be camera-shy. It was on the TV in the day room. And speaking of the day room..."

He opened a door and we entered the room I'd seen on the monitor in the receptionist's office. It was a large room and had probably functioned as a dining room when this building had been built.

Now, it was furnished with card tables and a large TV bolted to the wall. There was a buzz of activity at the tables where card and board games were being played. The TV droned at a low volume and there was a low hum of chatter as cards were dealt and dice were rolled. The only other sound was the constant pitter patter of the rain against the windows.

Three men in white uniforms stood discreetly at the edges of the room, arms folded, eyes alert.

"This is the day room where visitors and residents can relax," Campbell said. We have patients who visit the hospital when they need to attend therapy sessions and others who are residents here. This is where Ryan and Joanna met. At the time, Ryan was a resident and Joanna was visiting us for therapy. They discovered that they had something in common; apparently both of their great-grandparents came from the same small village in Scotland."

"What village is that?" Felicity asked.

Campbell closed his eyes and appeared to be searching his memory for a moment. At last, he said. "I believe it was a place called Aberfoyle."

"Aberfoyle," Felicity said. "I know that name from somewhere."

"Apparently, it's a small place," Campbell said. "So it was quite a coincidence. And that coincidence was enough to get them to talk to each other every time Joanna visited the hospital. After Ryan left here, they began dating."

"Against your wishes?" Felicity asked. "It sounds like you didn't approve."

"Miss Lake, when two paranoid people get together, they can sometimes feed each other's paranoia. I believe that's what Ryan and Joanna did. And then they brought their poor son into the world and kept him locked inside."

"He has a skin condition," I said.

Campbell nodded. "Yes, I know. Ryan had a similar condition, although his was far milder. He told me it runs through the male bloodline in his family."

A voice from one of the tables interrupted us. "I know you."

I looked over to a card table where a scrawny, bearded man was rising from his chair and pointing at me. He looked confused, as if he were trying to remember something. "I've seen you before," he said, coming toward me. "I've seen you somewhere before."

"It's okay, James," Dr. Campbell said. "You probably saw Mr. Harbinger on the TV today."

"No," James said. "Not on the TV. In my dream. You were in my dream."

Two of the white-uniformed men had unfolded their arms and were inching closer in case there was going to be trouble.

"You saw me," James said. "Don't you remember me? My name is James. James Elliot." A look of relief crossed his face. "You can tell them that I'm telling the truth. You were there too. In the shadow place. Tell them you saw me there." He was standing a couple of inches from me now, his dark eyes searching mine. "Tell them it's real."

The two security guards had almost reached him, were about to grab him. I raised my hand to tell them there was no need. There was nothing threatening in James's behavior, he just seemed confused.

"I don't remember you, James," I told him. "Maybe you can remind me where we met."

"Of course you remember. You must remember," he said, becoming anxious. "They don't believe me about the shadow place but they might believe you. You were..." He put the heel of his hand against his forehead, trying to force the memory to reveal itself. "You were in a house. I was in the street looking up at you. In the window. You were standing in the window. You and your black friend were standing in the window." He dropped his hand and looked questioningly at me. "Was it my house? Or was it your house? I can't remember."

I suddenly knew what he was talking about. Leon and I had been in a house in the Shadow Land, a shadow version of Blackthorn House, the house where the Bloody Summer Night Massacre had taken place and Mallory had become a final girl. We had looked down at the street from the window and seen a figure standing there. A figure that we were sure was...

"Mister Scary," I said.

James jumped back as if I'd swung a butcher knife at him He fell into the arms of a security guard. His eyes went wide and his face contorted in terror. "Don't say his name," he said. "Never say his name!" He looked at Campbell for support. "Doctor, tell him to be quiet. He has to be quiet!"

"All right, James," Campbell said gently. "I'm sure Mr. Harbinger won't say that again. Maybe you'd be happier in your room?"

James shook his head. "No, I'm fine." Shaking off the security guard, he stalked back to the card table, casting a glance over his shoulder in my direction. "You should have told them," he said. "You should have told them I'm not crazy."

"We should leave," Campbell said. "I'm sorry your visit ended on a sour note." He ushered us out of the day room and into the corridor. "How did you know that James has an irrational fear of Mister Scary?"

I couldn't exactly tell him that I'd seen James in the Shadow Land. Instead of believing that his patient was telling the truth about being there, Campbell would instead decide I was in need of therapy myself or that I was humoring James by confirming his story. I shrugged. "Just a lucky guess."

He didn't seem satisfied with that answer and he

watched me through narrowed eyes. "I think the real answer may be less dependent on luck. You obviously know James, which is why he recognized you, and you knew what to say to trigger a reaction from him."

"Why would I want to trigger the guy? He was terrified. I wouldn't do that to him on purpose."

"Well, all I know is that now we're going to have a hell of a time trying to keep him calm for the rest of the day. I'll show you out."

"Oh, but you said you'd show us why the hospital is called Butterfly Heights," Felicity said, giving Campbell a doe-eyed look. "I'd really like to know more about this place."

Campbell looked at her, took a moment to decide, and then sighed. "I guess I can show you quickly. It's this way." He turned on his heels and marched away along the corridor. I gave Felicity a clandestine thumbs-up. She'd just prevented us from being kicked out on our asses. And Butterfly Heights had suddenly become a place of interest.

If James had seen Leon and me in the shadow version of Blackthorn House, did that mean he was Mister Scary? But why had he reacted the way he had when I'd mentioned Mister Scary's name?

"Doctor, is James suffering from schizophrenia?" I asked, catching up with Campbell. "Is there a dark side of his personality?"

He looked surprised. "What? No, James's

personality doesn't have a dark side. The man wouldn't hurt a fly. Psychology isn't quite as simple as you seem to think it is, Mr. Harbinger."

"So educate me," I said. "Why did he react that way when I mentioned Mister Scary?"

"James believes that every night, he visits an otherworldly realm he calls the shadow place. He also believes that Mister Scary lives in the shadow place and hunts James whenever he sees him there. As you can probably guess, these are fantasies that James's mind has pieced together from real-life events."

He unlocked a door that opened onto the back of the property. A short flight of stone steps led down to a gravel path that wound through a walled garden to a rear gate. The gate was identical to the one at the front of the facility and was locked with the same type of electronic mechanism.

"James told me about the house and the two figures in the window a couple of weeks ago and he's been obsessing about it ever since," Campbell said, descending the steps. The rain had stopped falling but the grass and fallen leaves were slick with water. "It's probably a dream he had, based on a memory from his childhood, I'd guess. Maybe he was in the yard one day, looked up and saw his parents arguing near the window. Those kinds of events can have a long-lasting effect on children. In James's mind, it has become an event that happened recently, in the shadow place."

Leading us to the gate, he said, "And the Mister Scary of James's dreams is merely a personification of his troubled mental state in the guise of a real-life killer who is at large in the world." He pointed through the gate at a meadow.

Overgrown with wild grass and dead plants, it didn't look like anything special.

"It doesn't look great at this time of the year," Campbell said, "but in the summer, that meadow is full of wild lupine, vibrant with purple spires. The plants are the breeding ground of the silvery blue butterfly and thousands of them come here every summer. So the building is named Butterfly Heights."

"Interesting," Felicity said.

"Well, I suppose you'll want to be on your way," Campbell said, starting back toward the building. "It's a long drive back to Dearmont. I'm sorry I couldn't have been more help but I hope I've shown you that we deal with some very complex patients here and that Ryan Martin's death was a result of his illness."

"You're sure he's dead?" I asked as we walked back along the patch.

"Unfortunately, yes. There is no way a man with Ryan's problems could survive for two years without medical help."

I realized Felicity wasn't walking with us. I looked back and saw her standing at the gate, staring at the overgrown meadow. "Felicity, you coming?"

She turned to face me and began walking along the path to catch up. "Yes, of course." I could tell by the look in her eyes that she was thinking about something. "Dr. Campbell," she asked as she reached us, "what was this building called before it was named Butterfly Heights?"

He frowned at her and said, "It's been called Butterfly Heights since the day it was built."

"I see." She didn't seem satisfied by his answer but didn't pursue the matter.

We followed the doctor back inside, through the corridors and locked doors, until we reached the reception area. Steve was sitting at his desk, watching the monitors with a bored expression on his face.

Dr. Campbell shook our hands. "I'm sorry you didn't get the answers you were looking for but in a case like Ryan Martin's, sometimes there aren't any easy answers. If his body had been found, then maybe Joanna could have had some closure but there's probably no hope of that now. Tell her that if she feels she's losing control, she can make an appointment to see me." He turned and walked back into the facility.

Felicity and I walked to the door but Steve's voice stopped us. "Could you sign out, please, Mr.

Harbinger?" He was at the hatch with the clipboard in his hand.

I made a note of the time we were leaving in the appropriate column and signed my name.

Steve squirrelled the clipboard away and said, "I'm sorry you didn't find what you were looking for today."

"Actually," I said, walking to the door, "we found much more."

9

When we got back to the parking lot, the rain had started falling again. Felicity had been quiet during the walk back along the path and I could tell her mind was mulling something over. As we climbed into the Land Rover, I said, "What's on your mind?"

"Dr. Campbell is lying to us."

"About Ryan Martin?"

"About the building. He said it's always been called Butterfly Heights but that can't be true. According to the date on the stone over the door, it was built in 1894."

"They didn't have butterflies in 1894?"

She shot me a look. "Of course they had butterflies but they didn't have lupines. Not here, anyway. The lupine was introduced to Maine in the 1950s, so Campbell's story about the lupine meadow attracting silvery blue butterflies and giving the building its name in 1894 is hogwash."

"So maybe he doesn't know the building was called something else before it was Butterfly Heights."

"Perhaps not," she admitted, "but I think there's more to it than that."

"What do you mean?"

"I have some suspicions about the building but I need to do some research to confirm them."

"Okay, and what do you think of James Elliot? He seems to have some sort of connection to Mister Scary. Leon and I were in Shadow Land and we looked out of a window and saw a figure, just as James described. We thought we were looking at Mister Scary."

"Maybe you were mistaken and it was James."

"The guy we saw was holding an axe. I'm sure it was Mister Scary."

"So do you think they're the same person?"

I shrugged and started the engine. "I don't know. According to what Gloria told me, some people with a mental illness have a close connection to the Shadow Land. James might know what happened there because he saw it in his dreams or something but that doesn't necessarily mean he went there in person."

I backed out of the parking space and headed toward the main road. "I think we should stick around for a while until we find out more about Ryan's disappearance and James Elliot's connection to the Shadow Land."

"Sounds like a good idea," Felicity said, "but I don't think Dr. Campbell is going to let us into Butterfly Heights again."

"We'll find a way to get the information we need. We always do, don't we?"

She grinned. "Yes, we do."

"So let's book into that lodge for a few days and set up our base there. Then we can decide what we're going to do next."

"Sounds good."

We drove into Greenville and followed the signs to Lake Shore Lodge. They directed us to a large rustic building by the lake with a gravel parking lot that was mostly empty. I parked the Land Rover close to the door we ran through the rain to get inside but we still got soaked.

The foyer of the lodge was high-ceilinged with comfortable-looking chairs and low wooden coffee tables huddled by a huge stone fireplace in which a fire crackled and lent the room a pleasant woodsmoke smell.

Behind a long reception desk stood a white-haired man in his sixties. When he saw us, he pointed at us. "Don't tell me. You're newlyweds who want a romantic lake shore cabin for a week."

"No," Felicity said, smiling, "we're not."

His eyebrows wrinkled and he donned a pair of reading glasses to consult a piece of paper in front of him. "You're not Mr. and Mrs. Swain?"

"No, I'm Miss Felicity Lake and this is my colleague, Alec Harbinger. I booked two rooms for tonight."

"Colleagues?" He shook his head slowly and muttered, "I could have sworn you were the newlyweds. I have a nose for romance."

"You don't have a nose for anything, Marv," a large white-haired woman said as she came through an open doorway and joined him behind the counter. "Especially romance." She turned to Felicity. "Forty-two years we've been married and he hasn't given me flowers since 1983. Now, what can I do for you folks?"

"I was seeing to them just fine," Marv said.

"No, you were seeing romance where it doesn't exist." She consulted a computer. "Now then, Miss Lake, we have two rooms for you just for the one night, is that correct?"

"Actually," Felicity said, "we'll probably be staying longer than that. Will that be a problem?"

"If you're going to stay for a week or longer, you can have one of our log cabins at a good price," Marv said.

His wife shot him a look. "Marv, I'm dealing with this." Turning back to Felicity, she said, "But he's right, if you're staying here a while, you can have one of the cabins. We aren't busy this time of the year, to be honest, and they're just sitting there empty. You'll get a nice view of the lake and more privacy than if you stay here in the lodge."

"That sounds perfect," Felicity said, handing over her credit card.

"Just like that," Marv said, looking at me with a twinkle in his eye. "She didn't even consult you, mister."

"She's in charge of this side of the business," I told him, wondering how the Society was going to react when it received an expense claim from Felicity for a week's stay in a lakefront cabin.

"Oh? And what business are you in?" he asked.

"Preternatural investigation."

He cast me a knowing wink. "Tracking down ghosts, huh? Who you gonna call?"

"That's right," I said.

"Well, I don't really believe in that kind of thing but if it makes you a buck or two, then more power to you. What are you doing in Greenville?" He looked around the foyer. "You don't think the lodge is haunted, do you?" For someone who was a self-professed non-believer, Marv seemed pretty worried all of a sudden.

"I don't think so," I said. "You heard any strange noises at night?"

"No chance of that around here," Edith said. She slapped Marv's arm. "And you snap out of it. Of course the lodge isn't haunted." She took a set of keys from a peg and handed them to Felicity. "Follow the sign that says *Cabins* out of the parking lot and after a quarter mile or so down the road, you'll see a sign that says *Pine Hideaway*. It's the first cabin you'll come to. I hope the weather clears up some for you while you're here."

We left the building, got in the Land Rover, and drove along the road until we found the *Pine Hideaway,* a solid-looking log cabin that had two levels with large windows looking out over the lake. Wooden decking ran around the side of the cabin that faced the water and there was a little gravel beach and a wooden dock. Tall pine trees provided privacy from the lodge and the other cabins.

"How lovely," Felicity said, getting out of the Land Rover and running through the rain to the cabin door.

I went around to the trunk and took out our cases. I suddenly realized how hungry I was. I hadn't eaten since early this morning and that was a long time ago as far as my stomach was concerned.

I hauled the cases into the cabin. It was spacious, neat, and basic with a sofa and two armchairs in the living area. A large fireplace and a stack of firewood dominated one wall and a wood stove sat in the corner by a dining table. The air was lightly scented with the smell of pine.

Felicity came out of the kitchen, where I could

see a four-burner stove, microwave, fridge, and coffee maker. A flight of wooden stairs led upstairs to the bedrooms.

"The sight of the kitchen has made me hungry," Felicity said. "I haven't eaten since breakfast."

"I was just thinking the same thing." I was going to ask her if she wanted to come to the store with me to get some food but I noticed her shivering from the cold. "I'll head out and get some supplies."

"All right," she said, smiling. "I'll get the fire started. It's a bit cold."

"Any requests?" I asked her as I dropped the cases and went back to the door.

"No, just get what you think we'll need. You know what I like."

"Tea and cakes," I said. "Gotcha."

"There's no need to get any tea," she said. "I've got about a hundred tea bags in my case."

"I should have guessed," I said, going back out into the rain. "See you later."

I drove into Greenville and found a convenience store that sold groceries, beer, wine, and gas, as well as pizzas and subs. Since I had no idea how long we'd be staying at the cabin, I got enough groceries for a couple of days. I also got two large pizzas, some beer, and a bottle of wine.

By the time I headed back to the cabin, the smell of melted cheese and hot pepperoni drifting from the pizza boxes on the passenger seat was driving me crazy with hunger.

My phone rang just as I reached the Lake Shore Lodge parking lot, the caller's number unknown. I parked the Land Rover and answered it. "Harbinger."

"Mr. Harbinger, it's Dr. Campbell at Butterfly Heights Hospital." There was a touch of anxiety in his voice, just enough to let me know he hadn't wanted to make this call but had been forced to for some reason.

"How can I help you?" I asked him.

"Well, it seems your visit today had quite an impact on James Elliot. He's managed to lock himself in one of the storerooms and he's refusing to come out unless he can speak with you."

"On the phone?"

"In person."

"Okay, I can be there in half an hour."

There was a pause, and then he said, "I thought you would be on your way back to Dearmont."

"I'm in Greenville at the moment."

Another pause and then, "All right, let's see if we can resolve this situation quickly. Then we can all get back to how things were before you arrived at Butterfly Heights."

"Half an hour," I said, ending the call.

When I got back to the cabin, there were fires blazing in the fireplace and the wood stove. The slightly sweet smell of burning birch wood hung in the air.

Felicity appeared from the kitchen, saw the pizza boxes in my hands and grabbed them, sliding them onto the dining table. "They smell amazing!"

"Yeah, but we don't have much time to eat them. We need to go back to Butterfly Heights."

"Back to Butterfly Heights?"

"Dr. Campbell called me. James has locked himself in a room up there and won't come out until he can speak to me."

"Oh no, I hope he's all right."

"Me too. I guess we'll know when we get there."

"The pizza can wait."

"I was thinking the same thing. We can grab a slice for the road and eat the rest later."

We wolfed down a slice each on the way out of the cabin and climbed into the Land Rover.

10

Dr. Campbell led us along a corridor past the day room to an unmarked door. Two security guards were leaning against the wall, looking bored.

"James," Campbell called through the door, "Mr. Harbinger is here as you requested. So you can come out now. Everything is going to be okay."

"Mr. Harbinger?" James called. "Are you really there?"

"I'm here, James. And call me Alec. What's the problem? Why have you locked yourself in there?"

"They wouldn't let me call you. After you left, I saw you on TV. You were helping a woman whose son was attacked by a monster, because that's what you do, right? That's your job?"

"That's right. I'm a P.I. A preternatural investigator. I help people who are in trouble."

"I told them I wanted to call you but they wouldn't let me."

"We can't let our residential patients call just anyone," Campbell said to me in a low voice.

I turned my attention back to the door. "What do you want to talk about, James?"

"I want to hire you. I need your help."

"What do you want me to do?"

He didn't say anything but slid a piece of paper under the door. I bent down and picked it up. It was neatly folded in half. When I unfolded it, I saw a charcoal drawing of a dark, menacing figure holding a meat hook. The face was a simple black oval with no features at all.

"I want you to kill him," James said through the door. There was a pause and then he added, "He makes me see things I don't want to see."

"James," I said, "you don't have to hire me to kill him. I'm already looking for him. He hurt someone I care about."

"You mean Mallory," James said matter-of-factly.

That took me by surprise. "Yes, Mallory. Do you know her?"

"He doesn't know her personally," Campbell whispered to me. "He knows the details of all the Mister Scary murders, the names of the victims and the survivors."

"Mister Scary doesn't like Mallory," James said.

"He doesn't like her at all. I've seen her in the shadow place too."

"She's in the shadow place?" Could that explain why I hadn't been able to contact her or was this just part of a fantasy James had created? I had no way of knowing but based on the fact that James seemed to be able to see things that happened in Shadow Land, I couldn't afford to ignore this new information.

"Please tell me you aren't buying in to this," Campbell said. He sighed and shook his head. "Bringing you here was obviously a mistake. I thought we could get James out of there without the use of force and maybe learn something that would aid in his treatment but you're just fueling his delusional state."

He turned to the guards. "Break down the door."

"I'll get the battering ram," one of them said, pushing away from the wall and sauntering away.

"James," I said, "you should come out. They're going to break the door down. I promise I'll help you if I can."

Silence.

"James?"

"He does this sometimes," Campbell said. "He'll probably sink into a depression and stay quiet for a few days."

"Is there anything in there he could use to hurt himself?"

He shook his head. "No, it's an old storeroom.

We haven't used it for years. That's how he was able to get the key unnoticed. No one even knew it was missing. He's probably had it for a while, waiting for the right time to use it."

The guard returned with a metal battering ram. "Stand back," he said. He swung the ram at the door and the wood splintered but the door remained closed. "These old doors are tough," the guard remarked. He swung the ram again. This time, the lock broke and the door flew open.

The room was in darkness. By the light spilling in from the corridor, I could see shapes beneath sheets, shelves running along the walls. The dry smell of dust was almost choking.

The guards rushed in and I heard James shout out as they grabbed him. They dragged him out of the room and into the corridor by his arms. His eyes were wild and scared. "Kill him!" he shouted at me. "I don't want to see those things anymore!"

"What things?" I asked, stepping forward. "What does he show you? And what do you know about Mallory?"

"That's enough, Mr. Harbinger," Campbell said, putting a hand on my shoulder. "Entertaining James's delusions isn't helping anyone, certainly not him."

I shrugged his hand away. I wanted to say more to James but the guards had roughhoused him through a door and locked it behind them.

"It's time you left," Campbell said. "Bringing you here was a mistake."

"We're leaving," I told him, "but you need to listen to me first. What James is experiencing is more than just a delusion. You're treating him as if everything he tells you is a fantasy or a repressed childhood memory but there's more to it than that. You need to consider other possibilities."

Campbell sneered. "What—that he's telling the truth? That he travels to a shadow world where a serial killer resides? He guessed correctly when he thought he'd found an ally in you. But you have to believe every monster tale that comes through your office door, I suppose. It's all in a day's work for you."

I didn't bother to reply. I turned and stalked back to the exit.

When we were back inside the Land Rover, the rain drumming on the roof, Felicity studied the picture James had given me.

"We'll never get a positive ID from that," I said, pointing at the black oval James had drawn instead of a face.

"I wouldn't be so sure," she said. "The face may be missing but there's something else here that confirms my theory about Butterfly Heights."

"Oh? What's that?"

"The hook."

"The hook?"

She nodded. "I need to check a couple of things

on my laptop so I can be certain but I think I know what Butterfly Heights used to be called and what happened there. It may also explain what's happening to James."

I started the engine. "Okay, let's see if you're right."

During the journey back to the cabin, the picture of Mister Scary lay in Felicity's lap, the featureless face staring up at me.

I wondered if we were finally going to catch the murdering son of a bitch.

11

The evening was getting gloomy when got back to *Pine Hideaway*. I threw a fresh log on the fire and opened a couple of beers while Felicity sprawled out on the rug in front of the fire and opened her laptop and began punching the keys.

I brought the pizzas over to the coffee table and ate and drank in silence, giving Felicity space to do her thing.

"I knew it," she said after five minutes. She sat up and grabbed a slice of pizza, eating it while she made notes on a notepad.

I took a sip of beer, intrigued, but knowing I had to be patient. Felicity would tell me what she'd found once she'd organized her thoughts and was ready to reveal her discovery.

"Butterfly Heights," she said after taking a sip of beer, "was originally the Pinewood Heights Asylum.

Built in 1894 and operational until 1942, when it was closed down due to one of the patients murdering nine members of staff. The building was neglected for seventeen years until it reopened as Butterfly Heights in 1959."

She placed her laptop on the coffee table and turned it so I could see the screen. It showed a grainy black and white photo of a handcuffed man being led into a courthouse by police officers.

"This photograph was taken in 1929. It shows a man named Henry Fields. He was found guilty of the murder of nineteen teenagers between 1925 and 1928. He killed them with a meat hook and earned the nickname Henry the Hook. You know the urban legend of The Hook or The Hookman?"

"The one where two kids are making out in a car and they hear about an escaped convict on the loose and he has a hook instead of a hand? And when they drive home, they find a hook hanging from the car door?"

Felicity nodded. "Yes, that one. Some people believe that parts of that urban legend are based on Henry Fields." She put James's drawing of Mister Scary next to the laptop and pointed at the hook in his hand. "This is the person James sees in his dreams, the person he fears in the Shadow Land. It's Henry Fields."

I finished my beer and set the bottle down next to the pizza boxes. "But there's no face in the picture."

"There doesn't have to be. There's a connection between Henry Fields and James Elliot, and the connection is Butterfly Heights. In 1929, Fields was deemed insane and was sent to the Pinewood Heights Asylum."

"And James is there now and he's haunted by this." I pointed at the drawing. "A man with a hook."

"I think haunted is the proper word," Felicity said. "I don't think James is dreaming all of this, like Dr. Campbell believes. He's literally being haunted by Henry the Hook."

I pointed at the photo of Fields. "Did he die in the building?"

"Yes, he's the patient who murdered nine members of staff. When the police arrived, they discovered that after murdering the staff members, Fields hanged himself in the director's office. He'd carved occult symbols into his body and into the bodies of his nine victims."

"Which is what Mister Scary does."

Felicity nodded and took a sip of her beer.

"Okay," I said, "so what do we think Henry Fields is? A ghost? A demon?"

"I think it's much more complicated than that. It sounds like he performed some sort of ritual when he died. He's probably still alive, perhaps somewhere in the Shadow Land."

"There's probably a shadow version of Butterfly Heights," I said. "He's probably there. But how do we get there? The last time I was in the Shadow Land, Leon and I traveled there from Faerie."

"But you said Mister Scary used mirrors as portals to this world. Couldn't they also be used to travel from here to the Shadow Land?"

"Yeah, I think that's how he moves between different rooms of the houses when he's carrying out his murders. He goes back and forth between the real and shadow versions of the house he's in."

"If he can do it, so can we," she suggested.

I thought about it for a moment. It made sense but there were a couple of drawbacks. "We don't know how to open the portal. Leon and I cut our hands and placed them on the mirror in the shadow version of Blackthorn House but I think it only worked because the portal was already activated and had been used before. We have no idea how to activate a new portal."

I opened another beer. "And we'd have to use a mirror in Butterfly Heights. I have a feeling Dr. Campbell won't let us anywhere near the place now."

"The Blackwell sisters might know something about activating a portal to the Shadow Land," Felicity said. "And if we can break into Butterfly Heights without anyone knowing, we can use a mirror there."

"It would be risky. There's a lot of security."

"I'm sure we can come up with a plan."

I laughed. "You're very gung-ho about breaking the law. This isn't like you at all."

She shrugged. "This could be a real chance to catch Mister Scary. Think of how many lives we could save. Besides, it isn't like we're going to steal anything. We're just going to use a mirror for a while and then leave. No one will even know we were ever there."

"You make it sound so simple," I said.

"It is." She finished her beer. "I'll ring the Blackwell sisters and you work out a plan to get us inside." She got up and went to the kitchen. A couple of seconds later, I heard her speaking to Victoria Blackwell on her phone.

I mentally ran through a list of magical items I owned that could help us break into Butterfly Heights. There were some that could get us inside using force but smashing our way into the building would only get us arrested. We needed to ghost in and out of there undetected.

What we needed was a teleportation device but I didn't have anything like that. The last time I'd teleported anywhere was when the Blackwell sisters had sent me to a stone circle in England via an ancient spell. Unfortunately, their spell could only transport people to and from places of worship so it wasn't going to get us inside a mental facility.

Or was it? I went into the kitchen where Felicity was still talking and waited for her to pause. When she did, I said, "Ask Victoria if their teleportation spell would work with a chapel inside a hospital."

Felicity listened to Victoria for a moment and then said, "Yes, it would." Understanding dawned on her face and she said into the phone, "If there's a chapel inside Butterfly Heights, would you be able to get us in there?" She gave me the thumbs-up.

It stood to reason that Butterfly Heights had some sort of chapel within the building like most hospitals. If the Blackwell sisters could get us in there, Felicity and I could find a mirror and open a portal to the shadow version of the building.

I wandered back into the living room, thinking about the security I'd seen at Butterfly Heights. There were cameras inside and out so we wouldn't be able to move freely within the building unless we disabled them somehow. Another problem would be the digital locks on the doors but I was sure I had an item that would take care of those.

Felicity came into the living room. "Victoria said there's no problem getting us into a chapel inside the building but she's not sure how to activate a portal so they're going to look into it."

"Great. So we should be able to get inside just so long as the building has a chapel."

"I'm sure it has, considering it was built in the late nineteenth century." She threw another log on the fire, sat on the floor, leaning her back against the sofa, and opened a beer. "What's our next step regarding the Sammy Martin case?"

"I guess we should try to speak to local law enforcement, see if they'll tell us anything about Ryan's disappearance that Dr. Campbell may have neglected to mention. I'd also like to speak with the security team that followed Ryan to the storm drain that night."

"If that team includes Steve from reception, I don't think you'll get very far. He isn't very friendly."

"True, and I expect the police to be just as unfriendly. I assume there's a police department here somewhere so the officers who attended the scene would be based there."

"Yes," she said. "We're in Piscataquis County and the county sheriff's department is based south of here in a town called Dover-Foxcroft but there's a local police station here in Greenville."

I grinned. "You know everything, don't you?"

"No, not everything," she said, taking a swig of beer. "When you said we were coming to Moosehead Lake, I researched the area for anything that might help us with the case, such as the hierarchy of the local police. It's my job to know things."

"I couldn't work this case without you," I told her. "And tomorrow, when the Greenville police kick me out on my ass, I'll be relying on you to come up with a new plan to solve the case."

She laughed. "You don't know that they'll kick you out."

"Like I told you earlier, the police hate P.I.s. It's an occupational hazard. Well, it is for me, anyway."

"And as I told you earlier, not everyone hates you. I don't think even Sheriff Cantrell hates you, really. He just has some issues to work out regarding the death of his wife and his hatred of anything that could even be remotely called paranormal."

"I wonder how he is."

"Did you ring Amy?"

"I did."

"And?"

I sighed. "She told me to go to hell."

"Oh, that's a bit worrying."

"That she told me to go to hell?"

"No, that she's not keeping an eye on her father. We have no idea what Excalibur did to him. I hope he's all right."

"Look," I said, "Amy may have hung up on me but I'm sure she took what I told her seriously. She'll be watching over her dad, I'm sure of it. And I'm also sure that if anything weird happens, I'm the first person she'll call, even if it's just to bawl me out."

"I'm sure you're right." But Felicity looked worried.

"Did you find anything in the Arthurian lore?" I asked her.

"No, not yet. There's a lot to look at and with all

the research surrounding the case as well, I haven't really had the time."

"Not a problem," I said. "Mister Scary and Sammy Martin are our priorities. We'll deal with Cantrell if we have to but as long as everything stays quiet and we don't get a call from him or Amy, we'll put that problem on the back burner for now. Hell, for all we know, the sword didn't actually do anything to him."

"You said his eyes were glowing. That sounds like something."

"Okay, it's something. But right now we have to focus on Mister Scary and Sammy. We don't have the resources to work three cases at the same time and we don't even know that what happened to Cantrell *is* a case. Maybe he just had a bad reaction to the sword and that was that. It lasted a couple of minutes and then was gone."

But even as I said those words, I remembered the sword calling my name. For whatever reason, it had rejected me when I'd gone to it. The voice in my head had disappeared. But when the sword had been calling me, it had seemed to have a purpose for doing so.

And maybe, when it had reached into Cantrell's mind, it fulfilled that purpose.

12

Sheriff Cantrell drove his police cruiser into the parking lot of Darla's Diner and killed the engine. There were only a couple of other cars in the lot. The rain was probably keeping people indoors, warmth and a home-cooked meal more appealing than going out to eat.

Since leaving Harbinger's house earlier today, he'd felt lightheaded. The world around him seemed fuzzy and distant. And he couldn't hear anything clearly, as if his ears were stuffed with cotton balls.

Maybe a burger would fix that. It could be a blood-sugar thing. He'd been meaning to go to his doctor to get checked out for a while now but hadn't made the appointment, probably because he didn't want to be told he had a problem and that he had to change his diet.

It was getting dark. His shift was over but he

couldn't remember what he'd been doing for most of the day. He knew he'd been to the Martin residence and talked to the press, and then what? Had he been driving around town aimlessly? His mind couldn't recall any details.

His phone rang. It was Amy. He tried to shake the sudden tiredness he felt and sound upbeat. Amy could usually tell when something was wrong. "Hey, Amy."

"Hey, Dad, where are you?" She sounded concerned. Had she detected something in his voice?

"I'm at Darla's," he said.

"Oh, have you eaten already? I was going to make us something."

"Haven't eaten yet. Haven't gone inside yet." For some reason, it took effort to get each word out of his mouth. And he suddenly felt cold—very cold. The heater had switched off along with the engine but he shouldn't be feeling this cold yet. He felt as if he were encased in ice.

"Dad, are you okay? You don't sound too good."

"Not feeling great," he said. "I just need to eat, I think." He turned the car on again and as the engine came to life, he dialed the heating all the way up.

"You should get home. I'll bring you some chicken soup."

"Okay," he said through chattering teeth. Was he getting a fever? He pressed the back of his hand against his forehead. His skin felt frozen.

Then he heard a crackling sound all around him. Ice was beginning to spiderweb across the windshield and the windows, slowly at first but then faster. In a couple of seconds, it had covered every inch of glass.

"What the hell?"

"Dad, what is it? What's wrong?"

Although his view of Darla's Diner was obscured by the ice on the windshield, he could see no ice on the diner at all. And the other cars on the lot were unaffected. Only his car was affected by the ice. He tried to open his door, to get out, but it was frozen shut.

"Amy, I need help." He felt the ice creeping into his blood now, slowing his heart. He tried to breathe deeply, to get more oxygen into his system, but the air around him felt thin. He could see his weak breath misting in front of his face.

"Dad, what is it? Should I call an ambulance? I'm on my way."

"No ambulance," he said weakly. "Won't do me any good." This was no blood-sugar thing. It wasn't anything normal and thinking otherwise wasn't going to help him or Amy. He remembered what Harbinger's assistant had said earlier. "Blackwell sisters," he told Amy. "Get...Blackwell...sisters. Only they can...help me."

His brain was too cold to conjure up any more words and his lips were too numb to speak them. He closed his eyes, expecting to fall into a long, deep sleep. But instead of seeing darkness, he saw a vision.

It was as if he were entombed in a slab of ice that sat within a cave and he was looking up at a ceiling of dirt, rocks, and huge twisting tree roots. He couldn't move, couldn't breathe, couldn't cry for help.

Cantrell opened his eyes again and saw the interior of the car. Ice was now creeping over the steering wheel, the dashboard, the seats. The vision was somehow manifesting itself in the car.

He closed his eyes again and saw the vision of the cave, tried to dismiss it from his mind. He couldn't.

When he tried to open his eyes again, he couldn't.

His eyelids were frozen shut.

Amy Cantrell arrived at Darla's Diner, the lights on her patrol car illuminating the building with flashes of blue. A handful of people had gathered around her dad's car. Why were they just standing there? Why weren't they helping him?

Throwing open her door, she dashed from the car and pushed her way through the gawkers. When she saw the car, she stopped in her tracks and felt a fist grip her heart.

The patrol car was sheathed in ice. It clung to the doors, the windows, and the tires. There was no ice anywhere else in the parking lot and even the ice that surrounded the car had only spread for a few feet in each direction.

She could see her dad inside, sitting behind the wheel. He wasn't moving.

"Somebody call an ambulance!" she shouted at the people standing there. But no one moved.

Amy realized that the bystanders were just as frozen as the car. There was no ice anywhere near them but they were frozen in place, their eyes staring blankly at the patrol car.

"What the hell is going on here?" Her question drifted into the cold night, unanswered.

Turning back to the car, Amy tried the door. It was frozen shut. She pulled on the handle with all her strength but she couldn't get a grip on the ice-coated metal.

She remembered that she needed to call an ambulance. Grabbing her phone from her jacket pocket, she began punching in the numbers but stopped when someone spoke behind her.

"There's no point in calling an ambulance, Amy. It won't help your father."

Amy whirled around and found herself facing Victoria and Devon Blackwell, the two people her father had said could help him. Both women were wrapped up against the cold in long black coats that reached down to their ankles and thick black scarves that wound around their necks and trailed down to their knees.

"What's happening?" Amy asked. The words came out weaker than she had intended; she mentally cursed herself for sounding like a lost child in front of these two women whom she hardly knew.

"We aren't exactly sure," Victoria said. "Devon had a vision of your father in trouble so we came here immediately." She gestured to the frozen car. "And we found this."

"Is he dead?" Amy asked.

"No," Devon said. "But he needs our help."

"Now, why don't you go into the diner and find some hot water so we can get the car door open?" Victoria said to Amy.

Without hesitating, Amy sprinted to the diner. The place was empty, all the staff and customers outside by the car. Had they been affected by the same thing that had frozen her dad's car?

She found two empty coffee pots and filled them with hot water, careful not to spill them as she went back outside. When she reached the car, she poured the water over the edges of the driver's door.

The ice cracked and softened. Amy pulled on the door and it opened. When she saw her dad, she was sure he was dead. His skin was blue and he was completely covered in a layer of frost.

She reached in to unbuckle his seatbelt but Devon gently pushed her aside. "Let us handle this.

It could be dangerous to move him without the proper precautions."

Amy did as she was told, wondering why she was even listening to these witches. Maybe she should call an ambulance, let the medical professions help her father. But the last thing her dad had said to her on the phone was to get the Blackwell sisters. He usually dismissed the sisters as phonies or kooks, so there must have been a good reason for him to ask for their help. Amy just prayed she was making the right decision by honoring his request.

"We'll get to the bottom of this," Victoria told Amy. "Don't you worry."

Devon reached into the car and closed her eyes.

"What is she doing?" Amy asked.

"She's just trying to find out what has happened to your father."

"And what about these people?" Amy indicated the diner's staff and customers who seemed to be frozen in time. "Did the same thing happen to them?"

"Oh, don't worry about them, dear. We did that. We couldn't have all these poor people confused about what they saw tonight, could we? Things like this can give a person nightmares. After we leave here, they'll all wake up with a slight hiccup in their memories. They'll probably wonder why they're standing out here in the parking lot but apart from that, they'll be right as rain."

Devon, eyes still closed and one hand pressed against the sheriff's forehead, said, "He's under an enchantment. His mind is locked inside a dream. There's a cave deep beneath a tree and there's someone else in there with your father but I don't know who it is."

"There, you see," Victoria said to Amy, "paramedics couldn't help him with that, could they?"

"But you can?"

Victoria smiled warmly. "We'll do everything we can to help. I think it's safe to move him now."

Devon opened her eyes and nodded. "He's deep within the dream. He won't wake up."

"Waking him up could be quite traumatic," Victoria explained. "Come on, dear, help us get him to our car."

Between the three of them, they got the sheriff out of the car and carried him across the parking lot to a black Volvo station wagon. When she felt her dad's frozen skin beneath her fingers, Amy found it hard to believe he could still be alive. He was so cold that a chill emanated from his entire body.

They managed to get him onto the back seat of the Volvo. Seeing him lying there, Amy felt a stab of grief. Her dad was usually so strong and healthy. She'd seen him show weakness a couple of times since her mom died but he'd never looked as fragile as he did right now in the back of the Blackwell sisters' car.

"We need to hurry," Victoria said, pointing at a thin layer of ice that was beginning to spread over the seat around the sheriff. "If we don't get home in time, our car will freeze up."

"I'll follow you," Amy said, rushing back to her patrol car. She realized as she got behind the wheel that she wasn't exactly sure where the Blackwell sisters lived. She knew it was a house somewhere out of town but she couldn't remember ever actually seeing it.

The Volvo roared to life and tore out of the parking lot. Amy started the patrol car, floored the gas pedal, and skidded out onto the highway. She hit the lights and turned on the siren. There probably wouldn't be much traffic around but whatever there was would get out of the way.

She followed the Volvo north on the highway for a couple of miles and then along a side road through the woods. The rear window of the Blackwells' car was frosted over and Amy could see a sheen of ice glinting on the bodywork. She had no idea how far it was to the witches' house but she hoped they got there before the ice reached the Volvo's engine and froze it.

"If that happens, we'll just put Dad into my car," she told herself. "We'll get there okay." She wasn't even sure where "there" was or what the Blackwell sisters could do to help her dad but she couldn't let herself think about that. She had to concentrate on the task at hand or she'd go crazy and, right now, the task at hand was to get to the Blackwell house before the magic ice, or whatever the hell it was, made the Volvo's engine seize up.

A couple of minutes later, the Volvo's blinker came on, indicating that it was about to make a right turn. Amy knew this stretch of road and she knew there was no right turn ahead. Were the witches pulling over? Maybe the car couldn't go any farther. She put her foot over the brake, ready to slow down and pull over behind the Volvo.

But the witches didn't pull over. The Volvo made a right turn into the trees. Amy's heart leaped into her mouth as she watched the black car head straight toward a seemingly impenetrable wall of tall pines.

"No," she shouted. The Blackwells must have lost control of the car. They were going to crash.

But the Volvo drove into the trees and disappeared, as if the wall of pines was nothing more than an illusion. Amy hit the brakes and the patrol car skidded to a stop. She turned the wheel in the direction of the trees and inched forward. The pine trees loomed large in the windshield but she kept going, slow enough that if she hit a solid trunk, her car wouldn't be a write-off.

Just as she was sure she was about to crash into a tree, the hood of her car vanished and met no resistance. Amy continued forward, watching as more of the car disappeared into what was obviously some kind of mirage. When she was through the illusory trees, she found herself driving on a short road that led to a house.

The Volvo was parked in front of the house and the Blackwell sisters were pulling Amy's dad out of the car, which was now completely covered in ice.

Amy pulled up behind the Volvo and jumped out of her car, helping the witches to get her dad into the house. They took him down a flight of stairs into the basement and through a door into a room that was bare except for a cot and magical symbols painted on the walls and floor in various bright colors.

When the sheriff was on the bed, Victoria said, "The enchantment won't be able to spread beyond this room." She put a hand on Amy's shoulder. "He'll be safe here with us, dear. Now, let's get you a nice cup of herbal tea."

"But what's going to happen to him?" Amy asked as Victoria led her upstairs to the main part of the house. "How are you going to help him? How long will it take?"

"We'll find out what sort of enchantment has got a hold on him and we'll try to remove it," Victoria said as they entered a bright and airy farmhouse-style kitchen. She lit a gas stove and put a kettle on the burner. "Now, if we only knew how he became enchanted in the first place, our job would be much easier. Has he been antagonizing any local spell-casters? Reading books about black magic without taking the proper precautions?"

"What? No, nothing like that. He doesn't read books about magic and the only local spell-casters around here are you and your sister."

Victoria nodded, frowning. "Never mind, we'll find out where the enchantment came from. It would just be quicker if we had more information."

Amy remembered her conversation with Alec Harbinger earlier. "Wait a minute, Alec Harbinger may know something. He called me today and said my dad had been mesmerized by a magical item or something."

Victoria's face brightened. "Oh, Alec knows. That's wonderful. We'll get to the bottom of this in no time, I'll just give him a call." She took a phone from her jacket pocket and began tapping on it. Bringing it to her ear, she said, "Alec, how are you, dear? Oh, that's good. Listen, we have a small problem here. Sheriff Cantrell is under some sort of enchantment and his daughter said you might know something about it. Something about a magical item."

She listened and nodded and then said, "I see. No, no, it's nothing to worry about, we have the matter in hand." She stopped and listened again and said, "He's in an enchanted sleep. At our house. Yes, Amy is aware. She helped us bring him here. No, there's no need for you to do anything, dear, Devon and I will sort it out. Okay, bye."

She put the phone away and said to Amy, "Alec says your father has been enchanted by Excalibur."

"Excalibur? What do you mean?"

"It's a sword that King Arthur—"

"Yes, I know what Excalibur is. I mean how did it put a spell on my dad?"

"The sword is at Alec's house. Your father was there and somehow ended up in the basement with the sword. And his eyes were glowing."

"What?" Amy couldn't believe what she was hearing. Was her family forever doomed to be affected by the paranormal events in this town? "There's something you can do, right?"

Victoria nodded but her former confidence had disappeared. "It may take a little longer than if this were a regular enchantment. Excalibur is a powerful magical artifact and whatever spell it has your father under will be difficult to break."

"So you can't help him?" Amy felt as if the world had suddenly become much darker. First her mom had been killed helping a P.I. investigate a black magic cult and now her dad had been put into an enchanted coma by Excalibur. He was lying in the basement of the house she now stood in but there was nothing she could do to help him. She was totally reliant on the witches and that didn't sit well with her.

"I didn't say that," Victoria said. "I said it would take a little longer, that's all." She began fussing with the kettle and spooning herbs into a mug. When she was done, she handed Amy a steaming mug that smelled of mint, lavender, and something Amy didn't recognize.

"What's in this?" she asked.

"Just some herbs from our garden," Victoria said. "Drink up."

Amy took a cautious sip. The drink was pleasant-tasting and warmed her insides immediately. "It's good," she said, taking another sip.

Victoria smiled. "And good for you. Now, it's going to take us a few days to find out exactly what is ailing your father but you can come here and visit him anytime you like."

Amy nodded, wondering how she was going explain her dad's absence at the station. She was going to have to tell everyone he was sick. She didn't like the idea of lying to her colleagues but she could hardly tell them the truth, that her dad been enchanted by King Arthur's sword. It sounded ridiculous even to her and she'd seen the strange ice that had emanated from his body, had seen the Blackwell sisters' Volvo freeze with her own eyes.

"Are you all right, dear?" Victoria asked.

"Yeah, sure. I'm just worried about my dad, is all."

"Well, that's understandable but rest assured that

Devon and I will do all we can to wake him up. We'll get him on the road to recovery in no time, I'm sure of it."

"Okay," Amy said, unsure why she trusted the witches but unable to deny that she did. "I should get back to the diner, deal with my dad's car, create a cover story."

"I'm sure it will have thawed out by now," Victoria said. "The freezing effect is centered on your father's body so as soon as we took him from the car, the ice would have started to melt."

"Aren't you afraid it will freeze your house?"

"The enchantment can't escape that room. There are hundreds of years' worth of wards protecting the rest of the house from whatever happens to be in that room. Now, let's get you to your car."

Amy followed her outside to the clearing in which the house was situated. Before she got in to her car, she turned and looked at the rambling house with its steep gables and arched windows. She'd never heard of this house, even though it was only a couple of miles north of town. She wondered if the illusory wall of trees was the only privacy measure set up around the building.

"You're wondering why you aren't familiar with our house, aren't you?" Victoria said.

"Yes, I am," Amy admitted. "Can you read minds too?"

"Not at all, that's Devon's gift. But it's obvious

that someone who has lived in this area all their life, as you have, would be surprised that this house exists. As far as you were aware, there was nothing out here but woods."

"I assume it's hidden by spells. But why the need for secrecy?"

A sad look entered Victoria's eyes. "There was once a time when people like us were persecuted."

"But those times are gone."

"True, but this house has been here a long time and so have the spells that protect it."

"I can understand wanting to protect your family," Amy said. "My dad is the only family I have left. Please protect him too."

"Of course," Victoria said.

Amy got into her car and drove along the short road to the illusory trees. The last thing she saw before she passed through the spell was Victoria Blackwell watching her with a concerned look on her face.

When she got to the highway, Amy pulled over and put her face in her hands, letting the tears she'd refused to shed in front of the Blackwell sisters flow freely. She'd been forced to put her dad's life in the hands of two witches because whatever was affecting him was way outside her experience.

Nothing in her training as a deputy had prepared her for the paranormal events she'd had to face since Alec Harbinger had come to town, and she hated him for it. Worse, she hated herself for being so useless where the paranormal was concerned.

She'd taken this job to help people but in a world of monsters and witches and enchanted swords, how could she hope to make a difference?

Wiping her eyes, she got back on the highway and drove toward Darla's Diner, all the while thinking about her dad lying on a bed in the witches' basement, surrounded by ice.

13

I woke up to the sound of rain lashing against the cabin window and the tantalizing smell of bacon in the air. I dressed quickly and went downstairs to find Felicity in the kitchen, spatula in hand, making breakfast. Two frying pans sat on the stove, one full of sizzling sausages and rashers of bacon, the other loaded with fried eggs. A mound of toast sat on a plate on the counter, next to a full pot of coffee.

"I thought the smell of bacon might bring you running," Felicity said as I stumbled bleary-eyed into the kitchen.

I grinned at her. "You know me too well. Anything I can do?"

"You can pour the coffee." She began transferring the food from the pans to the plates.

I poured myself some coffee and added creamer and sugar. "You having tea?" I asked her.

"No, I'll have coffee today."

I poured another mug and followed Felicity into the living room, to the small dining table that sat in the corner. She placed the plates on the table and I set the coffees down next to them. "It smells delicious," I said, sitting down.

Felicity sat down and reached for her coffee. She drank most of it before touching the food on her plate.

"I'll get the pot," I said, heading back into the kitchen. When I got back to the table, her mug was empty. "I didn't think you liked coffee much," I said, pouring a refill for her.

"I don't, but what Victoria told us about the sheriff worried me. I spent most of the night researching Excalibur to see if I could find out what it did to him. I didn't get much sleep."

"You didn't have to do that, Victoria said they have everything under control."

"I know but I can't bear to think of Sheriff Cantrell under an enchantment. He isn't the nicest man in the world, I know, but I wouldn't wish that on anyone."

I knew what she meant. The Blackwells were taking care of the sheriff but I felt a little responsible for his condition. He'd been at my house when the sword had enchanted him and he'd only been there because of my involvement in the Sammy Martin case. "Did you find anything?" I asked Felicity.

She shook her head and sighed. "Not really. I can't find anything in the lore that mentions Excalibur putting anyone into an enchanted sleep. There's no precedent for it as far as I can see."

"Why would it do that to him?" I said, taking a bite of toast. "And why Cantrell?"

"I don't suppose we'll know that until we find out what it's actually done. I just hope Victoria and Devon can bring him out of it."

"I'm sure they can," I said. "They may be eccentric but when it comes to magic, they know their stuff. But I guess this means we'll have to do our own research into opening a portal at Butterfly Heights. The witches will probably be too busy."

"I can look into that," Felicity said, finishing her second coffee. She began eating her breakfast, her actions slow and thoughtful. I guessed she was already working on the portal problem in her head.

"Hey," I said, "do you want to stay here when I go to the police station? You could probably use some rest."

"I'm fine. The coffee should kick in soon. And I'd like to see the town."

"Even in this weather?" The rain was still lashing against the cabin, and through the windows, I could see dark clouds hanging over the lake.

"I'm from England, remember? I'm used to the rain."

I couldn't argue with that. We ate breakfast in

silence while the rain drummed against the windows. When I pushed my empty plate away, I said, "That was amazing. I could get used to having breakfast with you every morning."

That hadn't come out as I'd intended. "What I mean is—"

"It's fine," Felicity said, putting her hand on mine. "I know what you mean." She collected the dishes and took them to the kitchen quickly. I heard her fussing around in there, washing the dishes and putting them away.

Way to go, Harbinger, I told myself.

I got up and went to the kitchen, where Felicity was putting the plates into a cabinet.

"Felicity, what I said just now...I didn't mean to suggest anything."

She closed the cabinet and looked at me. "I know you didn't. It's just that being here with you —*living* here with you—brought back some of the feelings I was experiencing before I went to England and it's making me feel a bit awkward. I don't want there to be any awkwardness between us."

"Me either," I said.

"Perhaps this cabin wasn't such a good idea."

"It's a great idea," I said. "I like spending time with you. I'm sorry I opened my big mouth. What I meant to say was that breakfast was great. That's all."

"You didn't mean anything else?" She was asking

a genuine question, not accusing me of overstepping some boundary that might exist between us.

"No," I said. Although now that I thought about it, maybe my comment had been a Freudian slip. Being here with Felicity, seeing her first thing in the morning and getting to talk with her before starting work, was awesome.

I'd been keeping my emotions in check because of the conversation we'd had some time ago about keeping our distance from each other. God, that conversation seemed like it was a lifetime ago now.

"Okay," she said, taking the knives and forks from the drainer and putting them into the drawer.

Did she sound disappointed?

"Do you want to talk about it?" I asked.

"No, it's fine." She picked up the last plate from the drainer and began wiping it.

"If you want me to go stay at the lodge with Marv and Edith—"

She laughed. "No, there's no need for that. That would be silly when we have this lovely cabin. Besides, I don't think you'd be able to stand it there for long. Marv would probably hire you to bust some ghosts."

I grinned. "I'd have to get some coveralls and a proton pack."

"I could just imagine you dressed up like that, prowling around the lodge with Marv next to you, asking if you could hear any weird noises."

"And Edith saying there's no chance of that around here."

Her laughter became uncontrollable and she leaned her hip against the counter for support, removing her glasses so she could wipe tears from her eyes. The plate slipped from her hand and hit the floor, smashing into a dozen pieces that went skittering across the linoleum.

"Are you okay?" I asked her, moving forward to pick up the pieces.

Felicity nodded and mock-scolded me. "Look what you made me do!"

"I didn't do anything," I said innocently. "You were the one imagining me as a ghostbuster."

We both laughed and then our arms were around each other and we were kissing. She tasted of coffee, sweet and rich.

When our lips parted, her breath whispered against my mouth, her dark eyes wide, still glistening with tears of laughter. "I didn't expect that to happen," she said.

"If you didn't want it to—"

"No, I wanted it to." She leaned forward and kissed me again, her hands gripping the muscles of my back, pulling me closer to her.

I had no idea how long we'd been standing there, locked in an embrace, when a knock sounded on the door.

"Who can that be?" I said.

"It's probably Marv coming to request your services as a ghostbuster."

I groaned. "It had better not be."

"You should see who it is," Felicity suggested.

"Yeah, I should." I went back into the living room and looked out through the window. Steve, the security guard from Butterfly Heights, was standing out there. He wore a dark orange slicker and a faded John Deere cap that was pulled down low on his head, rainwater cascading from the peak like a miniature waterfall.

I opened the door. "Steve."

"Mr. Harbinger," he said. "I'd like to talk with you, if I may."

"Sure, come in."

He stepped inside and reached into the slicker, producing a large white envelope. "I have something you might be interested in." He handed it to me.

Felicity came in from the kitchen. "Would you like a coffee, mister...?"

"Waylon. Steve Waylon. You can call me Steve, miss, and coffee would be great. It's nippy out there this morning."

I opened the envelope and slid a sheaf of papers out of it. They seemed to be photocopies of Ryan Martin's records from Butterfly Heights.

"I shouldn't be giving you those," Steve said, "I could lose my job and much more just for copying them, but something has to be done and Dr. Campbell is ignoring the problem."

"Something has to be done about what?" I asked him.

"The problem at the Heights. I told Campbell ages ago that we needed to get a P.I. to look into it but he told me I was being ridiculous. I let it go at the time but when you came to the Heights and I saw that you were a P.I. I called Campbell and told him he should hire you. He refused."

Felicity came back with a mug of coffee and gave it to him.

"Thank you," he said. "So after Campbell refused to hire you, I thought that if I gave you what you wanted, you might help." He pointed at the papers in my hand. "Those are Ryan's records. They should tell you everything you need to know about Ryan, his problems, and maybe why he killed himself that night."

"You think he killed himself?"

He shrugged. "I think it's the obvious answer. He was very disturbed." He took another sip of coffee. "So now that I've given you those, will you help me with my problem?"

"What problem is that exactly?" I asked.

"The Heights," he said. "It's haunted."

"That's understandable," I told him. "A tragedy happened there some time ago and something like that can lock certain energies into the atmosphere."

"I don't mean ghosts. It's more than a ghost." He took a sip of the coffee. "Something weird happens there. You'd have to see it for yourself."

"Dr. Campbell won't let us near the place."

"I can get you in there after he's gone home. He works until late most days but I work shifts, so sometimes I'm there all night. Please say you'll take the job. If I have to deal with it much longer, I'll lose my mind and end up as a patient."

"Take a seat," I said, gesturing to the sofa. "I need to know more about what's happening. Is it connected to what James Elliot said about being shown things he didn't want to see?"

Steve sat down and put his mug on the coffee table. Felicity took a seat in the armchair and I noticed she already had her notebook in hand, pen poised over the page.

"Not exactly, no. But it affects everyone at the Heights," Steve said. "The patients and the staff. We have a huge turnover of personnel because no one wants to work there for long. The residential patients don't get a choice, of course, so they have to endure it."

"That can't be helping them with their problems," Felicity said.

"No, it isn't, it's making them worse. They already have a problem separating fantasy from reality so if they experience something weird, it just gets chalked up as a hallucination when they mention it in their therapy sessions."

"What exactly are they seeing?" I asked.

He frowned and stared at the coffee table for a moment before replying. I could see he was remembering something he'd rather forget.

"It's a song," he said. "A sad song without any words. Just notes being sung by a woman's voice. It comes from nowhere and it moves around the building."

"Sounds like typical ghostly activity."

"If you listen to it for long, it gets inside your head, makes you see things."

"What kinds of things?"

"Images. Visions. I don't know, it's hard to explain because the memory of what they were fades after a while."

"It could be a ghost showing you things from its previous life," Felicity said. "Perhaps it's someone who was a patient when the building was the Pinewood Heights Asylum."

"Yes, the old Pinewood Heights Asylum," Steve said. "That's what I told Dr. Campbell. I said it's probably something that's been around since then. There are terrible stories about the old asylum. He told me I must be imagining it."

"So Dr. Campbell knows the building used to be called Pinewood Heights?" Felicity asked.

He nodded. "Of course. The place was infamous.

Everyone knows what the Heights used to be called and what happened there."

"Yet Dr. Campbell told me it's been called Butterfly Heights since the day it was built," she said. "Why would he do that?"

Steve shrugged. "I have no idea. He knows all about the Pinewood Heights Asylum."

"Has Campbell heard the ghostly singing?" I asked.

"He says he hasn't."

"Are you particularly sensitive to the paranormal?" I asked him. "Have you seen or sensed things before? Things that other people didn't know were there?"

"Perhaps when you were a child," Felicity added.

"No," Steve said. "I don't see things that aren't there. The patients have heard the song too, and so have other members of staff."

"I don't mean it isn't there," I assured him, "just that you may be more sensitive to that kind of thing."

"It's real," he said. "Everyone hears it except Campbell. Come to the Heights tonight and you'll hear it too."

"We'll be there," I said. "What time?"

"I'll call you when Campbell leaves."

"Okay." We exchanged business cards. "And thanks for these." I held up Ryan Martin's records. "I know you're risking a lot by giving them to me."

"I'm trusting you not to tell anyone about them."

"Sure, no problem."

He got up and went to the door. Before he left, he turned to us and said, "If that ghost isn't stopped soon, it's going to make everyone in Butterfly Heights go crazy. I hope you can help us."

"I'll try," I told him.

"Thank you, I'll call you later." He gave us a brief nod and then stepped out into the downpour.

I turned to Felicity. "That solves the problem of getting into Butterfly Heights."

"Shall I look through Ryan's records while you're visiting the police station?"

"I thought you wanted to come with me, see the town?"

"That was before we got the records. I think the connection between Ryan's disappearance and the creature that attacked Sammy might be in these pages somewhere."

After what had happened in the kitchen, I hoped there wasn't another barrier being erected between us. "Okay, no problem. I'll go ahead and visit the police and you see what you can find in here." I placed the papers on the coffee table and put my boots on.

Felicity began arranging the papers into various piles on the table. As I shrugged on my jacket, I saw that she had three piles, one consisting of Dr. Campbell's notes from Ryan's therapy sessions, another of the drawings Ryan had made as part of his therapy, and a third pile that seemed to be made up of everything else.

"Is that a family tree?" I asked, pointing to a sheet of paper on the miscellaneous pile.

"Yes," she said, looking up at me over her glasses, "and it goes all the way back to the beginning of the last century."

"I wonder why that's in there."

"Many mental illnesses can be inherited," she said. "I assume this was used to track the history of Ryan's illness. A couple of the names are circled." She placed a hand on Campbell's notes. "The answer is probably in here."

"I'll leave you to it, then. See you later."

She waved at me distractedly but she was already concentrating on the records again.

I went out into the rain and climbed into the Land Rover, wondering if I should call Mrs. Martin to see how she and Sammy were doing. But I didn't have any progress to report regarding the investigation into her husband's disappearance so maybe I should wait until later. Felicity might find something in the records or the police might tell me something that would help.

As I started the engine, I grimaced at that last thought. It was more likely that the police would kick me out of the station. As far as they were concerned, Ryan Martin's disappearance was a two-year-old case that was best forgotten—just a patient from the local mental hospital getting himself killed in a storm drain.

They didn't want a preternatural investigator snooping around and asking questions.

"Everybody hates P.I.s," I told myself as I backed out onto the road and drove through the downpour toward town.

14

———————

I found the police department easily. Greenville wasn't big enough to get lost in and the building that housed the local police force was just off Moosehead Lake Road, the main road that ran through town.

I parked outside the small building just as a deputy was coming out. He came over to the Land Rover and I wound down the window.

"Can I help you?" he asked.

"I was hoping to talk to someone about a disappearance that happened here a couple of years ago."

He looked over the Land Rover and my face with searching eyes. "You the press?"

"No. I've been hired by the wife of the person who disappeared."

"You mean that fella from the hospital up on the hill?"

"That's right. Is there someone I could talk to about what happened?"

"There's nobody here but me and I wasn't involved in that case."

"Do you know who was?"

He nodded and as he did so, the rain poured from the brim of his hat. "The deputy on duty that night was Mike Taverner. The reason I remember that, even though it was two years ago, is because Mike left his job the day after."

"You mean he retired?"

He shook his head and more water flew from it. "No, Mike was a young man. I'm not going to stand here in the rain and tell you about his business. If you want to know what happened that night, you'll have to talk to him. But he never told any of us what made him quit so I can't see him telling you, a total stranger."

"Do you know how I can contact him?"

He looked me over again, sizing me up. "I'll tell you what I'll do. I'll call him and let him know you're looking for him and what you want to talk about. Then he can decide if he wants to talk to you or not, Mr..."

"Harbinger," I said, giving him my card.

He looked at it briefly before squirreling it away inside his jacket. "Preternatural investigator, huh?"

I nodded. "That's right."

"Well, I'll tell Mike you want to talk to him but I

can't see him talking to someone like you. He doesn't believe in any of that stuff."

"Still, I'd appreciate it if you'd give him my number."

"I'll do that. You have a nice day, Mr. Harbinger." He turned away from my window and got into his car.

I guessed that the chances of Mike Taverner contacting me were slim so I might as well head back to the cabin and help Felicity with the records. I'd probably just get in the way, though. She seemed to have a system when she was researching and I'd probably wreck it if I started picking up papers and swapping them into different piles.

I was thinking about taking a drive along the lake road when my phone rang. It was Felicity. I answered it immediately. "Hey, what's up?"

"Oh, I didn't think you'd answer, I thought you'd be talking to the police. I was going to leave a message."

"No, the police thing was a bust. You find anything?"

"Yes, I think so."

"On my way."

15

When I got back to the cabin, I discovered that Felicity had arranged the photocopied records into a new order, with some of the pages seemingly discarded beneath the coffee table while others, including the family tree, were spread over the sofa.

She came into the living room from the kitchen, holding two steaming mugs of coffee. "I thought you might want a hot drink after being out in the rain."

"You must have read my mind," I said, taking one of the mugs from her. "It looks like you've been busy."

"I've gone through most of the notes and I think there are some things in these documents that could explain what happened to Sammy."

"Great, hit me with it."

"I had a look at the family tree," she said, picking it up from the sofa. "As you can see, the names at the top of the tree, the ones that date back the furthest, have the word Aberfoyle written beneath them."

I nodded. "The village in Scotland where Ryan's and Joanna's ancestors lived."

"That's right. I remembered why the name was familiar to me. It's where Reverend Robert Kirk lived in the seventeenth century."

"Okay, you've lost me."

She looked at me over her glasses. "You don't know who Robert Kirk was?"

I searched my memory but the name didn't appear anywhere in it. "No, should I?"

"Well, they teach about him at the Academy of Shadows but you probably didn't pay attention that day."

"Probably not," I admitted.

She sighed. "Robert Kirk was a folklorist and a minister based in Aberfoyle, Scotland. He wrote a book called *The Secret Commonwealth*. Perhaps you've heard of that?"

"Yeah, I've heard of the book. In fact, I'm pretty sure I have a copy somewhere. It's a book about faeries, isn't it?"

"It's about the folk beliefs of the people who lived in the Scottish Highlands, particularly those who had the second sight. Kirk complained that the people in the area spent more time consorting with faerie lovers than attending church. However, he apparently spent most of *his* time on Doon Hill, a local mound where the faeries lived. When he died, that's where his body was discovered."

"Sounds like he may have been taken to the faerie realm."

"Yes, especially when you consider he made a will the day before he died."

"So do you think him going to Faerie has anything to do with our case?"

"Not directly, no. But it means there's documented evidence that the people of Aberfoyle had a close connection to faeries. And a lot of them had the second sight, which meant they were more in tune with the unseen realms. Both Ryan's and Joanna's ancestors came from there so what if some kind of strong connection with the faerie realm has been passed down through each family line and manifested in Sammy?"

I thought about that for a moment. If the people of Aberfoyle were known to have the second sight and if it could be passed down through the bloodline, then it stood to reason that both Joanna and Ryan could have inherited it, maybe enough of it to give them hallucinations. And those hallucinations had made them seek therapy at Butterfly Heights.

"So when Ryan and Joanna got together, it was the perfect storm for creating a gifted child," I said. "Sammy inherited the second sight from both his parents and he's probably been sensitive to the faerie realm all his life."

"Exactly," she said.

I nodded. "It makes sense. But it doesn't explain why Sammy was abducted by a shellycoat or why a shellycoat was following Ryan around and probably killed him."

"I have a theory," she said. "We know the Shadow Land is formed of thoughts and that certain people are more in tune with it than others. The story of the shellycoat has been passed down through the Martin family since Ryan's great-grandfather apparently saw one in Scotland. And we're assuming that the members of the Martin family were gifted with the second sight. What if those people, the ones who heard the story, were so in tune with the Shadow Land that their thoughts brought the creature into existence?"

"You mean they created the shellycoat with their minds after hearing a story about it?"

"It isn't without precedent," Felicity said. "Have you heard of a tulpa?"

"A being created from mental images. Sure, it's an old Tibetan belief."

"That's right. And you said yourself that you believed Mister Scary was using the power of his mind to create shadow versions of the houses he was going to target."

"So the members of the Martin family unwittingly created a tulpa over the years," I mused.

Felicity shrugged. "It's possible."

"Yeah, I guess it is. It's a good theory." It definitely made sense. "But why would the tulpa attack Ryan and Sammy?"

"Did it really attack them?"

"Ryan disappeared in a storm drain and his clothes were shredded. The shellycoat took Sammy from his yard and left him in a cave. So, yes, I'd say it attacked them."

She put down her coffee and picked up a number of drawings. "Look at these," she said. "They're Ryan's drawings of the shellycoat. According to what he told Dr. Campbell, Ryan had been seeing this creature for as long as he could remember. He began drawing it when he was a child, after he saw it watching him from the bushes at the bottom of his yard. Why would it wait all those years before attacking him when it could have done so when Ryan was a child?"

"I have no idea."

"And it took Sammy from his yard, true, but then it just left him in a cave. It seems like it didn't mean him any harm."

I wasn't so sure about that; the damned thing had almost drowned Sammy in Dearmont Lake. And he'd been terrified when it had carried him through the woods. "So what are you saying? That the creature is friendly?"

"Not friendly, exactly, no. But we might be misunderstanding its intentions."

"Its intentions seemed pretty clear to me."

She pursed her lips, thinking, and then said, "No, I'm sure there's more to it than that."

My phone rang, the number unknown. "Harbinger P.I."

"Mr. Harbinger, this is Mike Taverner. I got a call from an ex-colleague who said you were interested in speaking to me about an old case."

"Yes, that's right. Thanks for calling me back. Could we meet somewhere?"

"Do you know the Lakeshore Diner?"

"No, but I can find it."

"I'll see you there in half an hour."

"Great. How will I recognize you?"

"I'll recognize you, Mr. Harbinger. I checked out your website and I've seen your picture. Half an hour, Lakeshore Diner." He hung up.

"Another lead?" Felicity asked.

"Yeah, the police thing panned out after all. Do we have a website?"

She looked sheepish. "Yes, I thought it might bring in more clients."

"And there's a picture of me on it?"

"Research has shown that if people see a real face on a company's website, they are more likely to buy the company's services."

"It hasn't worked so far. Maybe it's putting off potential clients."

"Nonsense. You have a very friendly face. If I

didn't already know you, I'd definitely do business with that face."

"Uh, okay," I said.

Felicity flushed. "I didn't mean—"

"It's okay, I know what you meant." I put my boots on. "I'm going to meet the deputy who went out to Butterfly Heights the night Ryan disappeared. You want to come with?"

"I think I'll stay here and go through more of Dr. Campbell's notes." She picked up the papers and began arranging them into more piles.

I left the cabin and got into the Land Rover. According to the GPS, Lakeshore Diner was fifteen minutes away. It was north of town and located, as its name suggested, on the lakeshore.

When I got there, I parked in the busy parking lot and jogged through the rain to the door. The diner was bustling. The smell of fried onions and meat made my mouth water as I found a booth and sat down.

"What can I get you today?" a voice said almost immediately after I'd taken my seat.

A waitress whose name tag said *Cathy* stood by my table, order pad in one hand, pencil in the other.

"What's good here?"

She gave me a smile. "Everything, of course."

"Okay, what's especially good?"

"Our specialty is the Lakeshore Burger. That's a

cheeseburger with everything on it and it comes with fries and a soda."

"Sounds great."

She turned to leave but then I heard her say, "Hi, Mike. The usual?"

"You know me too well, Cathy. And this fella here is buying." He slid into the booth and looked at me across the table. His hair was mostly gray but he couldn't have been any older than thirty. He was dressed in a shirt, jeans, and leather jacket that seemed too big for his scrawny frame. "Mr. Harbinger, I'm Mike Taverner." He held out a hand and I shook it. His grip was weak.

"Thanks for meeting with me," I said. "Your colleague didn't seem to think you would."

"Ex-colleague," he corrected me. "I don't do that work anymore."

"Since the night Ryan Martin disappeared."

"That's right."

"Why is that?"

He looked out through the window at the lake and the rain and the dark clouds. "A lot of people have asked me that question. When I quit, they all wanted to know what had happened that would make me throw in the towel. I never told any of them, they wouldn't understand."

Cathy came over to the table, set down two sodas, and filled our coffee cups. I added creamer and sugar to mine and waited for Mike to continue.

"I couldn't tell any of them what I saw that night," he said after Cathy had left us, "because they'd think I was crazy. Hell, even I thought I was crazy. But two years have passed and I know that what I saw was real. I've come to terms with that but I still haven't told anyone around these parts about it."

"But you'll tell me?" I asked.

He looked closely at me and said, "I will but only if you promise to kill it. That's what you do, isn't it? You're a monster hunter."

"That's part of my job. So you're saying you saw a monster that night?"

"Will you kill it? I've been afraid for the past two years that the damn thing is out there somewhere, waiting for me. Because not only did I see it, it also saw me and there was hatred in its eyes." He looked out through the window again. "As long as it's out there somewhere, I can't sleep. I barely leave the house anymore."

"Maybe you should tell me exactly what you saw that night."

Cathy returned to our table with the food. As she set the dishes down, Mike and I were silent. When she was gone, and I was eating my fries, he said, "I was the only person on duty that night. A call came in that one of the patients from the mental hospital on the hill had escaped and had climbed into a storm drain. I drove out there, cursing my luck that it had happened on my watch. It was raining, you see, about as heavy as it is now, and the last thing I wanted to be doing was searching a storm drain for a mental patient."

He popped a couple of fries into his mouth and ate them before continuing. "When I got to the drain, there were three people standing there on the road. Two of them worked security at the hospital and the other guy was a doctor. One of the security guys had already been in the drain and he was covered with slime and God knows what else, which made me even more reluctant to go down there.

"Not only that, they had some scraps of the missing guy's clothing, so I was sure he'd snagged himself on something down there and had then been washed away by the pressure of the water. What else could rip his clothes like that?"

He sighed. "Anyway, I knew my duty so I got my flashlight and climbed into the drain. It was big enough and I got inside pretty quickly, before I had a chance to talk myself out of it. I was expecting there to be a whole lot of water in that drain but there wasn't much at all, despite the rain. I didn't know it at the time but the drain was blocked with debris somewhere farther along so most of the water wasn't reaching the part I was in."

"So Ryan couldn't have drowned," I said.

"Ryan—that was his name," he said as if suddenly remembering. "Ryan Martin. No, he didn't drown, I know that for a fact. Anyway, I searched the drain for maybe a half hour before I was ready to give up on the guy. It stank like rotten leaves and dead animals down there and all I'd found was more scraps of clothing. So I was wondering whether to go back to the place I'd entered or look for a different way out. There were inlet grates every quarter mile or so and I had passed one maybe a quarter mile back so I was expecting to come upon another pretty soon. I decided that as soon as I saw it, I was out of there."

He shivered slightly and looked out through the window at the rain falling on the lake. "I found the grate," he said, "and that's when I saw it. It was hunched over and at first I didn't know what it was. Then it was suddenly aware that I was in there with it and it kind of unfolded itself and stood as high as a man, probably higher. It had scales like a fish and big claws and these staring yellow eyes that looked at me with a look of hatred, like I already told you."

His hands had begun to shake at the memory and he put them beneath the table as if ashamed. "I screamed," he said, "and I got the hell out of there. There were iron rungs leading up to the grate and I must have gone up them like a squirrel trying to escape a wolf. I slammed my shoulder against the grate and, thank God, it flew open. I scrambled out and found myself in the woods. I was sure that thing was going to come out after me and drag me back into the drain.

"I ran faster than I'd ever run in my life. I ran so fast, I thought my heart would burst. I didn't stop until I reached the road and collapsed from exhaustion. Next thing I knew, I was being driven to the hospital by one of those security guys. The next day, the sheriff came to see me in the hospital and I quit right there and then. I couldn't tell him what I'd seen, all I could do was blubber like a baby. My view of the world changed that day, Mr. Harbinger. There are dark things out there, things that no man should ever face if he wants to live a normal life."

"You said you know for a fact that Ryan didn't drown," I said. "When you saw the creature, did you also see his body? Had it killed him?"

Mike looked at me with sadness and confusion in his eyes. "No, it hadn't killed him. I found scraps of clothing in the drain but the rest of it was hanging off the monster's body. It was wearing a torn shirt and what was left of a pair of jeans. That monster didn't kill Ryan Martin. It *was* Ryan Martin."

16

Mike took a swallow of coffee, the cup shaking in his hand. "I'm not crazy," he said. "I'm telling you, that thing had once been human. It had once been Ryan Martin."

I tried to absorb this new piece of information, fit it into what I already knew. Had Ryan become a shellycoat somehow? Was it possible? There were some creatures that crossed the divide between human and preternatural, like the werewolf, but I'd never heard of anyone transforming into a fish-like creature.

And if Ryan's transformation had been lycanthropic, like a were-creature, why hadn't he contacted his wife and son when he'd changed back into human form?

Unless the transformation had been one way only and he'd simply become a shellycoat forever. In that case, maybe taking his son from the yard had been his way of trying to reach out to his family. Who knew what had happened to his mind and how much of Ryan was still in there? Maybe taking Sammy had been a primal instinct the creature hadn't even understood on a conscious level.

"You believe me, don't you?" Mike asked.

"Yeah, I believe you." It felt right. Ryan had spent his life dreaming about a shellycoat, believing he was being followed by one all the time. Maybe he was aware of something inside his own psyche, something that would emerge later, and his awareness had manifested in visions and hallucinations of an external creature which was actually within himself.

I needed to get back to Felicity and tell her this new information. We needed to act on it. Because if the shellycoat was actually Ryan, and he had found his son after all this time, he'd probably do anything he could to take Sammy again, even if he didn't understand why he was doing so.

"Mike, thanks for talking with me," I said. "You've been a great help. And I can assure you that the creature isn't in Greenville any longer. You can sleep easy."

"You know where it is?"

I nodded. I had no idea how long Ryan had stayed in this area after his transformation but at some point, he had wandered south, maybe not even knowing why. It had taken him two years but he'd eventually found Dearmont and his family.

"You're going to kill it, right?" Mike said.

"I'm going to deal with it," I said.

"You mean kill it?"

"Not necessarily."

"No, that isn't good enough. You have to kill it. I'll pay you if that's what it takes. I'll hire you to kill it."

"I've already been hired," I told him. "The creature is part of a case I'm already working on. You can't hire me to do something that would conflict with my client's interests."

"It can't be in anyone's interests can be to keep that thing alive," he said. "How many people do you think it's killed? A creature like that ain't vegetarian. You can't just let it live."

He had a point. If the creature had killed anyone, then it was my duty as a P.I. to take it out. As a member of the Society of Shadows, I couldn't do anything else, I had to kill it.

I wondered how Sammy Martin was going to feel when he found out that his father hadn't died two years ago at all but had changed into a preternatural creature.

A creature that I had to kill.

17

I was still contemplating that when I got back to *Pine Hideaway*. I climbed out of the Land Rover and went into the cabin to find Felicity still poring over the papers that were now arranged into yet more piles. I wondered if she'd taken a break.

"Hey, I have burgers," I said, holding up a sack of food from the Lakeshore Diner.

"They smell good," she said, looking up from the page she was reading.

"They are."

"Oh, you've already eaten?" She looked disappointed.

"Just a few fries. I had them wrap up my burger to go and I got you one too."

She got up from the sofa and put her hands on her hips, stretching her back. "I need a break. Did you find out anything?"

"Yeah, let me get this food sorted out and I'll tell you all about it." I went to the kitchen and unwrapped the food, putting the burgers and fries on two plates. "You want a beer?" I shouted to Felicity.

"Yes, please."

I grabbed two cold ones from the fridge and returned to the living room with everything balanced precariously in my arms. Felicity took a plate and a beer from me and sat down on the sofa again. "So, what did you find out?"

I told her about Mike Taverner and his version of events.

She listened while eating her burger and when I'd finished, she said, "I've found out some things about the Martin family."

"What's that?"

She sorted through the pages until she found the one she was looking for, the Martin family tree. She laid it on the coffee table and pointed at one of the names near the top of the tree.

I leaned forward and read it. JOSHUA MARTIN. 1919-1927. ABERFOYLE.

"As you can see, he died when he was only eight years old. He suffered from the same skin condition that Sammy has: photosensitivity. He spent most of his life indoors. When he did go outside, he was wrapped in a coat, scarf, hat, and gloves, no matter the weather. What's interesting about Joshua is that everyone considered him to be gifted with the second sight. On the few occasions that he went outside, his favorite place to visit was Doon Hill."

"The place where the faeries lived," I said.

"That's right. Joshua said he could see and speak to the faeries at Doon Hill. He also said he spoke to them in his dreams." Felicity put the family tree on the table and held up her hands. "Now, what I'm going to say next might sound a bit weird but hear me out."

"Okay," I said, intrigued.

"I'm assuming Joshua had the second sight and an affinity with the faerie folk because faerie blood was introduced into the bloodline of the Martin family."

"You think someone had sex with one of those fish creatures?"

"It could have been hundreds of years ago, even as long ago as the seventeenth century when Kirk complained about the people in the area consorting with faerie lovers, but I think it happened at some point, yes."

"So that could be why the second sight runs in the family," I said.

"Perhaps there's a latent gene that gives certain members of the family the second sight. It also gives those people some sort of skin condition. The skin condition is the marker for people with the latent faerie gene." She turned the family tree around on the table so it was facing me. "Look at this. Joshua's and Ryan's names are circled. And so is Sammy's."

I considered that. "But those notes were made by Dr. Campbell. If he circled the names, wasn't he marking the family members who had the skin condition?"

"That's what I thought at first but there's something in his notes that didn't make sense until you told me about Ryan's transformation."

She searched through the paper until she found what she was looking for. "Here it is. During a therapy session, he asked Ryan if there were any relatives who had the skin condition. Ryan mentioned his son, of course, and said there was a family history of it, going back as far as anyone could remember. He mentioned Joshua and Dr. Campbell made a note in the margin that says: *Joshua and Ryan may be the same as Hunsaker.* I assume he's referring to another patient. Then, at a later date, he wrote another note: *Can the serum only cause a metamorphosis in certain people?*"

"Metamorphosis," I repeated. I pointed at the records. "Is the name Hunsaker mentioned anywhere else in there?"

"Not in these documents."

"How about a serum?"

"No, and that's something else I discovered by reading through these notes: this is not a complete set of records. There are many pages missing. Campbell refers to other notes written on specific dates and they aren't here."

"You think Steve only gave us some of the pages and kept others back?"

"I don't see why he would. He wants us to help him so why would he try to trick us?"

"I don't know. Maybe there's something going on at Butterfly Heights that's being recorded in a different set of notes that Steve doesn't want us to see."

"Or a set of notes he doesn't even know about," Felicity suggested. "I don't think Steve would hold anything back from us. He seemed genuinely scared of the ghost he described. I got the impression that he really does need our help."

"The alternative explanation is that Dr. Campbell is up to something that nobody else knows about."

"There are definitely more documents somewhere," Felicity said. "And assuming Steve gave us everything from Dr. Campbell's files, those documents are being kept somewhere else."

"We can snoop around tonight," I suggested.

"Sounds like a plan."

"In the meantime, I'll call Steve and see if he knows anything about this patient named Hunsaker." I took his card out of my pocket and dialed his number.

When he answered, it sounded like he was

outside. I could hear the wind blowing and the rain hitting something that might be a car. "Hello?"

"Steve, it's Alec Harbinger."

"Oh, hey, give me a minute." Half a minute later, I heard a door shut and the sounds of the wind and rain disappeared. "I was just getting my groceries into the house," he explained. "What's up? Did you find what you wanted in those..." He paused and then said, "Did you find what you wanted?"

That was another reason Steve probably hadn't held out on us where the records were concerned: he was taking a big risk giving them to us at all. Why would he try to trick us when we could simply report him and get him into a heap of trouble?

"It was interesting," I said. "I was wondering what you can tell me about a patient named Hunsaker."

"Geraldine Hunsaker?"

"I guess. Or anyone else with that name."

"She's the only Hunsaker I can recall," he said. "She was at the Heights maybe five years ago. Same problems and same therapy as the other patients. She was with us for about three weeks, I think."

"There's nothing that made her stand out from the others?"

He thought about that for a moment and then said, "No, nothing."

"Did she have any sort of skin condition? Photosensitivity maybe?"

"No, definitely not. She spent a lot of time in the gardens while she was here. She liked the butterflies, I remember that about her."

There was a pause and then he said, "Hey, now that I think about it, she did have some sort of a skin problem. It wasn't photosensitivity, though. I remember she was standing in the garden one day and the butterflies were fluttering up from the lupine meadow. Geraldine raised her hands above her head, as if she could catch them, and her sleeves slid back and there were patches on her arms where the skin was, I don't know, thicker or something. And it was cracked, like if you get hard skin on the soles of your feet. But this was on her arms."

"Do you know what happened to Geraldine?"

"No, like I said, she left after three weeks. I never saw her again after that."

"Do you have an address for her?"

"It'll be on file."

"We may need it."

"Okay. Hey, what's going on? Why the interest in Geraldine?"

"I don't know yet, it may be nothing. See you later."

"Later," he said.

I ended the call and told Felicity what Steve had told me.

"I have a feeling she went missing after she left Butterfly Heights," Felicity said. "If she had the same faerie gene that Ryan had, she might have turned into a faerie creature too."

She grabbed her laptop and opened it. "If she went missing, we won't need that address. The Society database has a list of missing persons." She tapped on the keyboard and waited a few seconds. "Yes, here she is. Geraldine Hunsaker disappeared from her home in Massachusetts four years ago. She was never found."

She looked up at me, the glow from the computer screen reflecting in her glasses. "Do you think I'm right? That some people have a faerie gene and they end up at Butterfly Heights before undergoing some sort of metamorphosis?"

I took a bite of my burger and chewed it slowly, my mind going over what we'd discovered. The new information raised a question: If Campbell knew that some people had a latent gene that could transform them into faerie creatures, what was he doing with that information?

I could think of a few possibilities but the one that concerned me the most was that he might be experimenting on these people. Without seeing his secret notes, we had no way of knowing.

"When Steve lets us into the Heights tonight, we'll find out exactly what's been going on up there. I have a feeling Campbell's interest in faerie genetics is more than just academic," I told Felicity.

"So do I," she said. "In fact, I'm wondering if he's

actively seeking people like Ryan Martin and Geraldine Hunsaker. He told us Butterfly Heights takes patients from other mental health facilities all over the country. Since most people who have a close connection with the faerie realm will experience visions and hallucinations, they'll probably end up in one of those facilities at some point in their life. It wouldn't be difficult for Dr. Campbell to have the ones he thinks are carrying the faerie gene transferred to Butterfly Heights."

The implications of that were worrying. I went to the window and looked out over the rain-swept lake. I had an urge to go to Butterfly Heights right now and confront Campbell but I knew that would be pointless. He'd just clam up and throw us out. I had to wait until tonight to find the answers.

Until then, I had no idea if the doctor was trying to help the people under his care or if something much more sinister was happening to the patients at Butterfly Heights.

18

Before Amy had a chance to knock on the door of the Blackwell sisters' house, it opened and Victoria said, "Come in, dear."

Amy stepped over the threshold. "I came by to see how my dad is." She'd spent most of the day covering for her dad; driving his thawed patrol car to his house and leaving it in the driveway, telling everyone at the station that he was sick, probably with the flu, and wouldn't be at work for some time, and taking on his workload and appointments.

The entire time, she'd expected a phone call from the witches, telling her that her dad was dead. That phone call, thankfully, hadn't come but that did nothing to alleviate her worry that he wasn't going to make it.

"We've made some progress," Victoria told her. "Come on, I'll show you." She took Amy to the basement and opened the door of the room where the sheriff lay on the cot among the magic symbols.

Amy went to the cot and looked down at her dad, feeling a lump form in her throat. He was still frozen, his skin blue and covered with a sheen of ice. "He doesn't look any better," she told Victoria.

Devon came into the room, looking exhausted. Her eyes were red-rimmed and Amy wondered if she'd slept at all last night. She hadn't slept herself, of course, but Devon Blackwell looked as if she were suffering from more than just a lack of sleep; she looked as though her energy had been dragged from her body.

"The ice completely covered the walls of this room last night after you left," Devon said. "Now, it's only a few feet around the cot."

"Did you do that?" Amy asked.

"No," Victoria said. "It did that all by itself."

"The enchantment is changing," Devon said, "Evolving. I've looked into your father's mind. He's gradually waking up."

Relief flooded through Amy. "That's good."

Victoria and Devon looked at each other uncertainly.

Amy's relief became confusion. "That's good, isn't it?"

"We're not sure, dear," Victoria said. "Your father has become magically bonded with another."

"What? What are you talking about?"

Victoria placed her hands gently on Amy's shoulders. "We'll tell you everything we know but unfortunately, that isn't much."

"The enchantment has bonded your father with another being," Devon said. "That being was locked inside a slab of ice within a cave. That's what all this ice is about. At the moment, your father is traversing two worlds, this one and the one where the cave is located. So parts of that world are leaking into this one. Since the bond was formed, the slab of ice that has been imprisoning the being in the other world has been melting within the cave. And that's why the ice around your father is melting too."

"What do you mean a being? A monster?"

"We really don't know," Victoria told her. "But when the ice melts completely, your father will wake up."

"But the enchanted bond between him and the other being will persist," Devon said. "Part of your father will still be locked within the cave."

"And part of the being in the cave will come to our world, inside your father's body," Victoria added.

Amy felt hot tears sting her eyes. She was never going to get her dad back. Part of him was going to be locked away in another dimension and the part of him that was here was going to be possessed by a monster from another world.

"Is there anything you can do?" she asked the

witches. "Please, I'll give you anything you want if you save him."

Victoria gave her shoulders a light squeeze. "My dear, I'm afraid it isn't that simple. If there was anything we could do to help your father, we would have done it already. The only thing any of us can do now is wait."

"Wait for him to wake up possessed by a monster?"

"We don't know that it's a monster," Devon said. "It isn't clear."

"Of course it's a monster. What else would take over someone like this?" She gestured to the ice. Her dad looked so helpless, immobile on the bed. All her life, she'd thought him strong. He was a big man and with his size came a strength that always made Amy feel safe.

Now, that was gone. He was gone.

Unable to look at him any longer, she fled up the stairs and out to her car, where she sat behind the wheel for a long time, weeping for her dad, lamenting what was lost and fearing the monster her father was becoming.

19

Felicity and I spent the rest of the day researching magic portals but we didn't get any closer to finding a way into the Shadow Land. When it finally stopped raining, we took a walk along the lake to clear our heads and get some fresh air. By the time we got back to the cabin, it was getting dark.

After taking off her boots, Felicity went straight to the sofa and opened up her laptop.

"Hey, you don't need to do that now," I told her.

"But if we don't find a way into the shadow version of the hospital, we won't know if that's where Henry Fields is hiding. And if he's Mister Scary, we're missing an opportunity to save a lot of lives. I don't like the idea of us wandering in there unprepared."

"What do you mean? That's my usual way of working."

She threw a cushion at me. I dodged it and it hit the wall.

"You know exactly what I mean," she said. "I like to be prepared, that's all."

"Or is it that you can't find the information on the portal and that's bugging the hell out of you?"

She crossed her arms and rested her head on the back of the sofa, looking up at the ceiling. "Yes, that as well."

"Maybe it's something that only Mister Scary knows how to do."

"Well, I'll be sure to ask him when I see him," she said.

"That may be sooner than you think." My phone had started ringing, displaying Steve's number. "Harbinger," I said as I answered it.

"We're good to go," Steve said. "Campbell left ten minutes ago. He went home early today."

"We'll be there soon," I told him. I ended the call and said to Felicity, "Let's go,"

We drove out to the parking lot in the woods and I opened the Land Rover's trunk. "You want a sword or a dagger?" I asked Felicity.

"I'll take a sword, please."

I handed her an enchanted sword in a leather scabbard, along with a crystal shard that would glow if it detected magic. She attached the scabbard to her belt.

I grabbed a sword and crystal shard for myself and picked up another item, wrapped in a cloth.

"The Janus statue?" Felicity asked.

"Yeah, if there's a portal already open in there somewhere, the statue will find it. It'll also open locked doors, which may be useful if we need to search Campbell's office for those missing records." I put the statue into a small backpack and threw a dagger in there as well for good measure.

I closed the trunk, slung the backpack over my shoulder, and we trudged along the muddy path through the woods to Butterfly Heights. The iron gate buzzed open before we'd even reached it. I guessed Steve was watching the gate on one of the many cameras.

He was waiting behind the hatch in the reception area when we got inside, a nervous look on his face.

"You okay?" I asked him.

"Yeah, I'm fine. It's just the night, you know? It makes me anxious sometimes. The singing is more spooky when it happens at night."

"Don't worry, we'll deal with it."

I pointed at the bank of monitors behind him. "I'm going to have to ask you to turn off the cameras for a while."

"Why?"

"Because while we're waiting, Felicity and I are going to take a look in Campbell's office."

His brow furrowed. "I don't know about that. What if he knows you've been in there? I'll lose my job for sure."

"Can I ask you a question?" Felicity said.

He nodded. "Okay."

"Why are you so worried about losing your job here if it's making you this anxious? Why don't you get a job somewhere else?"

"I've asked myself that question a thousand times," he said. "The answer is that it isn't just about me. I can't abandon the patients. I'm the only person who cares about tackling this thing. Campbell can't even hear it and the other members of staff either pretend it's nothing or they leave. If I left too, no one would care enough to hire people like you to deal with the problem and the patients would never get better."

"You did the right thing by bringing us here," I told him. "Letting us search Campbell's office is also the right thing to do."

He sighed in resignation. "Okay, okay. I'll turn off the cameras for a little while. All the patients are in their rooms anyway." He went over to his desk and hit a couple of keys on a keyboard. The monitors went dark.

"We're going to go to Campbell's office," I told him when he came back to the hatch. "If you hear anything strange, call me."

He nodded and then saw the sheathed swords

hanging from our belts. "Jesus, what are you going to do with those? You're armed for bear."

"Don't worry about that," I told him. We headed toward the door that led into the main part of the hospital.

"Wait a minute," Steve called, "you're going to need these." He tossed us a couple of keycards.

I looked at the plain white card and held it up. "Will this open Campbell's office?"

"No, only the doors in the corridors. All the other doors have traditional-style locks and keys." He held up a keyring crammed with keys. "Campbell has the only key to his office, though. And also the only key to the basement."

"The basement," I repeated. "Why would he have the only key to the basement?"

Steve held his hands up. "Hey, he runs the place. I assume he has personal stuff down there."

I looked at Felicity. "We need to go to the basement."

She nodded. "My thoughts exactly."

"Which way is the basement?" I asked Steve.

He sighed again, probably resigned to the fact that the chances of him keeping his job were getting slimmer every second Felicity and I were here. "Through that door, turn left, and go all the way to the end of the corridor. Campbell's office is upstairs —it isn't that empty room he took you to when you first came here. The stairs are near the basement door. You'll see them."

"Thanks, and remember, if you see or hear anything strange..."

"Yeah, I'll call you. But right now, I'm not sure what the point would be. I might as well just let the ghost take me."

"Don't worry," Felicity told him, "Dr. Campbell will never know we were here."

We opened the door and went through it into the corridor.

As we headed toward the basement, Felicity pulled her sword from its scabbard. The enchanted blade glowed bright blue, reflecting off her glasses and the corridor around us.

"You expecting trouble already?" I asked her.

"We have no idea what we're going to find in that basement," she said.

I thought about that for a moment and then drew my own sword.

20

At the end of the corridor, we came to the basement door. It was probably as old as the building itself and made of sturdy oak with a brass plaque at eye level that had the word *Basement* engraved into it. It seemed innocent enough. I tried the handle. Locked.

I unwrapped the Janus statue and held it up. The two bearded faces, looking in opposite directions, could find inter-dimensional portals and keep them open but the statue could also open mundane locks. The Latin words to activate the statue were inscribed on its base but I knew them well enough to recite them without having to read them first.

After I said the short verse, the lock on the basement door clicked and I tried the handle again. The door swung inward. Beyond, a set of stone steps spiralled down into darkness. I found a switch on the wall and turned on the lights. As they flickered to life overhead, they cast a weak glow over the steps. What was down there at the bottom of the spiral staircase was anyone's guess.

"I wonder how deep this goes," I said, suddenly realizing that I was whispering.

"The building sits on a hill, so it could be a long way down," Felicity whispered back.

I put the unwrapped Janus statue into the backpack and threw it over my shoulder. "We won't know until we take a look," I said, tightening my grip on the sword and stepping down onto the top of the spiral staircase. A sudden chill seemed to fill the air and I got the unsettling impression that something was waiting for me at the bottom of the steps, something that knew I was coming down to meet it.

Trying to shrug off the feeling, I continued down. "I think you're right," I told Felicity, "this goes down a long way."

We continued down the steps, the air getting colder the deeper into the hill we went.

"This is one hell of a basement," Felicity said. "Why was it built like this? It doesn't make any sense."

"I guess the people who ran Pinewood Heights Asylum back in the day needed it to be deep underground for some reason."

As we finally approached the bottom step, I could see an iron door set into the wall. It was probably locked but as I got closer to it, the lock clicked open thanks to the Janus statue in my backpack. I pushed the door gently and it swung open. The room beyond was pitch-black.

I reached into the room and felt along the wall for a light switch. When I found one and flicked it, an overhead light stuttered to life. I stepped into the room, followed closely by Felicity.

The walls and floor were covered with white tiles and an old wooden desk and chair sat by a second iron door on the opposite side of the room. There were no other furnishings but the room did have one other feature: a mosaic of red tiles in the shape of a magic circle high on one wall.

"I've seen that symbol somewhere before," I said, searching my memory. "It was on the uniforms of the Midnight Cabal soldiers we met on the island of Dia."

"Yes, it was," Felicity said, looking up at the symbol. "What does the Midnight Cabal have to do with this place?"

"I don't know," I said, pointing at the second door. "But I guess we need to see what's through there."

Felicity nodded and, swords in hand, we crossed the room to the door. Its lock clicked open as we got close enough for the Janus statue to do its job. I pushed the door and it opened onto a corridor that was lit by a row of lights hanging from the ceiling. The walls in here were concrete. Four iron doors were set into the walls on each side of the corridor, with a ninth door at the far end. Each door was numbered and had a hatch at eye level.

I removed the backpack from my shoulder and put it on the desk. These looked like cells and I didn't want the Janus statue to unlock the doors and release whatever was inside. At least not until we'd checked them out.

I went to the first door and slid back the hatch. The cell was no larger than ten feet by six, with a rusted, steel-framed bed inside but nothing else, and certainly no occupant.

We checked the remaining seven cells on the sides of the corridor. They were all exactly alike, all empty.

"Do you hear that?" Felicity said as we approached Cell 9.

I listened. There was a noise coming from beyond the door, a sound like birds fluttering.

We looked at the door and then at each other.

"There's something in there," Felicity whispered.

I stepped forward and tried to open the hatch quietly. But the metal grated noisily as it slid aside.

Unlike the other cells, which had each been lit with a light set in ceiling, this one was completely dark. I couldn't see anything in there but I could smell saltwater and there had been more fluttering when I'd opened the hatch.

Now, the occupant of the cell was quiet.

I could sense it watching me. I stepped back instinctively and closed the hatch.

"What is it?" Felicity asked.

"I don't know, but it definitely isn't a ghost. There's something alive in there."

"We shouldn't open the door until we know exactly what it is."

"I have zero intention of opening it right now," I assured her. "Come on, let's go and take a look at Campbell's office. Maybe we'll find something that will tell us what he's keeping captive down here."

We went back to the outer room and closed the iron door.

"We can't lock it," Felicity said. "Dr. Campbell will know someone has been down here."

"The Janus statue can lock it," I said, taking the magical item from the backpack. "I just need to recite the words of the incantation in reverse order." I had to read the inscription on the base of the statue to do that, so I held it up and read each word from the last to the first. The lock slid home with a click.

I wrapped the statue so it wouldn't lock the iron door at the bottom of the steps until we'd passed through. When we were standing on the bottom step, I unwrapped the statue to lock that door. After a leg-aching climb back up the steps, I locked the basement door in the same fashion.

We walked back along the eerily quiet corridor

until we came to the wide staircase that led up to the second floor.

"At least this isn't so creepy," Felicity said as we ascended the stairs.

She was right. This part of the building was spacious and airy, befitting of a Victorian building built on a huge budget. The stair carpet was dark blue with gray ivy leaf motifs. Wood paneling lined the walls and the banister was carved ornately into the likeness of intertwined vines. Paintings of rural scenes hung on the walls and expensive-looking dark blue drapes covered the windows.

The stairs led to a wide corridor with a number of dark wooden doors and the same ivy motif carpet. I found a door where the nameplate said *Dr. Robert Campbell* and used the Janus statue to open it.

Unlike the sparsely-furnished office Campbell had taken us to when we'd first arrived here, this room was lined with bookshelves crammed with textbooks and leather-bound tomes. A large mahogany desk sat by the curtained window, its surface buried beneath stacks of books and papers.

"No filing cabinets," Felicity said. "He must keep his records in another room."

"But I think we'll find what we're looking for in here," I said. "If there's a separate filing room, it's probably shared between the medical team. If Campbell has secret documents, he won't risk them being discovered accidentally. They'll be in here, in his personal space."

"Where do we start?" she asked, indicating the mess of books and papers. To someone as organized as Felicity, this office was probably a nightmare.

"Start with the desk," I said, using the Janus statue to unlock the drawers. "I'll see what's on these shelves."

She began rifling through the papers on the desk, reading them and putting them aside in the same order they'd been before she touched them. I checked the books on the shelves, looking for anything that stood out. Most of them were psychology textbooks but there was also a scattering of medical books that dealt with hematology and cell biology.

"Perhaps the documents aren't here at all," Felicity said. "If they're so secret he can't risk them being found, maybe he keeps them at his house." As she said this, she was opening the drawers and searching through their contents.

"Maybe," I said, "but his patients are here. And that...whatever it is...is in the basement here. I don't think he'd transport his notes back and forth. He'd probably think they're safe enough here. If I'm wrong, and we don't find anything, we'll just have to break into his home. I need to know how much of a part he played in Ryan Martin's transformation."

"I've found something," Felicity said, bringing a

leather-bound book out of a desk drawer. The book was stuffed with loose papers and was kept shut with a black ribbon that had been tied around the covers. Felicity showed me a red magic circle that had been stamped into the leather. "The Midnight Cabal," she said. "And here's another." She brought an identical book out of the drawer and laid it on a pile of papers.

"Anything else in there?" I asked as she examined the drawer again.

"Just these keys," she said, holding up a set of keys on a metal ring.

"I assume they fit the doors in the basement."

She nodded and picked up the backpack from the floor. She tossed the keys inside and slid the books in too.

We were way past the stage of trying to be stealthy. The Midnight Cabal was somehow involved with Butterfly Heights and the books Felicity had found would probably be useful to the Society of Shadows. Besides, we wouldn't have time to read through them even if we spent all night in here.

"I can't see anything else of value," Felicity said.

"Nothing on the bookshelves either. I think we've found what we were looking for."

She closed the drawers and I used the Janus statue to lock them and the office door once we were standing outside in the corridor. Campbell would realize the books were missing when he opened the drawer but there was no point in telegraphing the theft of his stuff. Let him wonder what the hell had happened.

As we were heading back downstairs, my phone rang. It was Steve.

"It's here," he said as I hit the speaker button so Felicity could listen in. "Reception area."

I ended the call and we ran down the stairs.

21

When we opened the door that led to the reception area, the first thing I noticed was a smell of saltwater hanging in the air, the same as I'd smelled in the cell downstairs. The second was a mournful song sung in a woman's voice coming from nowhere in particular.

Steve was in his office, pressed against the far wall, hands pressed over his ears. "You hear it, right? Tell me you hear it."

"I hear it," I said.

"Get rid of it," Steve said in a panicked voice. "Do something!"

I took out my crystal shard and held it up. It glowed brightly, indicating strong magic at work. But without the proper equipment, there was no way we would be able to see the ghost. And I hadn't brought any of my ghost-hunting stuff to Moosehead Lake, it was all back in Dearmont.

"You were right," I told Felicity. "We came unprepared."

"I can't hear anything," she said.

"You can't hear the singing?"

She shook her head. "No."

Steve clutched his skull. "It's getting inside my head. Stop it! Please, stop it!"

I had no idea what was happening to him but we had to get him away from the ghostly voice. "We need to get Steve outside," I said, running for the door that led to his office. He was huddled on the floor when we got to him.

"Make it go away," he whimpered.

"We're getting you out of here," I said. "Can you walk? We need to get you outside."

He staggered to his feet. His face was drawn, his eyes bloodshot. Felicity and I took a hold of each of his arms and threw them around our shoulders, supporting him as we left the office, and made our way to the exit.

"Almost there," I assured Steve as we got closer to the door. "Just a couple more feet and we'll be—" I stopped as an icy finger of pain slid into my head. I cried out and fell to the floor, holding my head as if that would take the pain away.

I heard Felicity's voice say, "Alec?" but I couldn't reply. The singing reverberated in my head, mournful and longing. Visions flashed into my mind. I felt as if I were underwater in a deep, dark ocean, saltwater filling my throat and lungs, a woman's face in front of me, watching me with cold eyes.

Then I saw an island in my mind's eye, an island with a pristine beach and palm trees atop rocky cliffs. There were more women here, walking along the bright white sand in flowing, diaphanous gowns that seemed to float in the air around them. And the women had wings of brightly-colored feathers that shone in the sun.

The image changed again, became a vision of ships in the distance. They were old ships, sloops and frigates with white sails that bore the red symbol of the Midnight Cabal.

I heard Felicity's voice again but it was more distant now, drowned out by the singing. And I was suddenly beneath the water again, drowning, being pulled down to a deep, dark, watery death. I could feel my life slipping away as the mournful song continued, twisting through my mind. And in front of me was the woman, seemingly in no need of life-giving air as she held me in her arms and watched me drown.

Then I was lying on the lawn of Butterfly Heights beneath a cloudy, starless sky. Felicity was looking down at me, her dark eyes filled with concern.

"Alec?" she said. "Can you hear me?"

"I hear you," I said, struggling into a sitting position. "But I've got one hell of a headache."

Steve was lying on the lawn a few feet away, eyes open, staring up at the night sky. He looked as bad as I felt.

"What happened?" I asked Felicity.

"You collapsed and started holding your head and writhing around, just like Steve. I had to drag both of you out of there."

"You didn't feel it in your head? You didn't see the visions? The woman's face?"

"No. I saw both of you in pain but nothing else."

"I saw a beach," I said, getting up. "And ships on the sea."

"It's always the same," Steve said, sitting up and rubbing his temples. "The sea, the ships, and the drowning. I told you, it gets into your head. It gives you nightmares. The images fade eventually but right now I remember that they are the same images every time. And I'm afraid that there'll be a time when I see them and I won't wake up afterward. I'll drown in the nightmare. The patients' conditions are being made worse by that thing." He got to his feet unsteadily. "There must be something you can do."

"We need to go back inside," I told Felicity.

"Not while that thing is in there," she said.

"It'll move on to other parts of the hospital," Steve said. "It doesn't stay in one place for long. It's probably moved to the patients' rooms by now."

We went back into the building warily. The reception area was quiet.

"I need to put the cameras back on," Steve said, "at least for a little while. If Campbell knows they were turned off for long, he'll get suspicious." He sat at his desk and began typing on the keyboard. The monitors flickered to life. "What the hell?"

"What is it?" I asked.

"I just saw someone walking around the corner there," he said, pointing at one of the monitors.

"A patient?" Felicity asked.

"Their doors are locked at night. There shouldn't be anyone walking around." He typed on the keyboard again, bringing up various camera angles. "Damn it, it's James. How did he get out of his room?"

The monitor showed James Elliot shuffling slowly along the corridor. He looked as if he might be sleepwalking.

"Where's he going?" I asked Steve.

He shrugged. "Who knows? I need to get him back to his room."

"We'll come with you," I said.

Steve sighed. "It'd be better if you stayed here. James gets agitated when you're around."

He had a point. I needed to know more about James's knowledge of Mister Scary but I didn't want to upset him.

"We'll wait here," I told Steve. He could help us gain access to James in the future. Better to earn his trust than piss him off.

He took two walkie-talkies from a shelf and handed one to me. "Keep in touch with this. You can tell me if James turns off that corridor."

"Okay," I said, sitting at the desk in front of the monitors. "We'll keep you updated." James was still shuffling along the same corridor, as if in a trance.

"I'd like to know how the hell he got out of his room," Steve said, taking a last look at the monitor before leaving the office and going through the door that led to the inner part of the building.

The walkie-talkie squawked, Steve's voice sounding distant through the crackling static. "He still in that same corridor?"

"Same corridor," I said. "I'll let you know if that changes."

"Do you think this is related to that singing you heard?" Felicity asked me, taking a seat at the other desk.

"I don't know. It could be or James might just be sleepwalking."

Steve appeared on one of the monitors, jogging along the corridor. I saw him raise the walkie-talkie to his mouth and then heard his voice coming through the one on the desk. "I think he's headed for the old storeroom again. That's where we usually find him when he goes missing. He doesn't have the key anymore but the lock is busted, so he won't need one to get in there."

As Steve had predicted, James opened a door and

disappeared from the camera's view. "He's gone into a room," I told Steve.

"Yeah, I saw him close the door behind him. It is the old storeroom. I'll get him back to his room and I'll be back in the office shortly."

I watched him on the monitor as he went through the same door James had used moments earlier.

Felicity had opened the backpack and was looking through one of the leather-bound Midnight Cabal books.

"Anything interesting?" I asked her.

"I'm not sure yet." She flicked through a few pages. "It seems the Midnight Cabal used the Pinewood Heights Asylum as a cover for something they were working on in the 1940s."

"Which was?"

"I'm not sure but it involved experiments in the basement."

"Experiments on the patients?"

She shook her head, scanning the pages of the book. "Experiments on a creature they'd captured. There are lots of technical notes here, most of them referring to some sort of serum they were developing. They called it Project Ligeia. Named after the Edgar Allan Poe story, I suppose."

"It's a good thing this place got shut down after Henry Fields went on the rampage," I said. "Who knows what they might have achieved if their project had remained operational?"

"After it closed down, they probably continued the same experiments somewhere else," she said, reading more of the book. "Or maybe they didn't. It seems there were nine members of the Midnight Cabal based here, working on the project."

"And Henry Fields killed nine members of staff," I said. "Maybe he did the world a favor by taking nine members of the Cabal with him when he killed himself. Maybe he destroyed Project Ligeia."

"Except he didn't actually kill himself," Felicity reminded me. "He may have killed nine members of the Midnight Cabal but only to further his own plans. He used them to escape this place and cross over into the Shadow Land."

She pulled a black and white photograph from the book and gave it to me. The picture showed a man hanging in an office, surrounded by dead bodies. The photograph was grainy but that seemed to make the scene even more grisly.

"Pretty gruesome," I said, giving it back to her.

Felicity took a closer look at the picture and held it up so I could see it again. "Look in the corner."

In the corner of the room, behind the desk that had belonged to the director of the Pinewood Heights Asylum, stood a tall, oval mirror with an ornate wooden frame that was adorned with carvings of vines and ivy, matching the bannister we'd seen earlier. On the top right corner of the glass was a dark smudge. When I looked closer, the smudge looked like a handprint.

"That's the portal he used to get to the Shadow Land," I said. "But he didn't physically step through it, he killed himself after activating it. So what part of him went to the Shadow Land? His spirit? His soul?"

"Probably his astral body," Felicity said. "Whatever ritual he performed must have required that he lose his physical body. I suppose that without it, he can live forever in whatever form he's taken."

"But when he kills, he's a physical person," I said. "The Bloody Summer Night Massacre wasn't carried out by a ghost or an astral being. It was a person who attacked those kids."

She thought about that for a moment. "Maybe he hijacks real people's bodies, possesses them so he can commit murder, and then returns to the Shadow Land in his shadow form."

That made sense and it explained why Mister Scary couldn't be killed by conventional means. "He's inside someone else's body when he commits his crimes. So if the body is killed, he simply removes it from the scene and hijacks a new person next time."

She nodded. "He can't actually be killed himself because he's a spirit, or a ghost, or whatever. He's only driving the body that carries out the massacre. And I think we know where he's finding the bodies. The patients here could never tell anyone what happened to them because their experience would be passed off as a delusion. The patients themselves might even believe it's just a part of their illness."

"So James wasn't watching Mister Scary in the Shadow Land through some sort of remote viewing; he was actually there. When Leon and I looked down from that window, it was James we saw standing there, and he was possessed by Mister Scary?"

Felicity's eyes were suddenly filled with concern. "Do you think he's forced James to murder people?"

I considered that. "Probably not. The last time Mister Scary struck, Leah Carlyle killed him, so that body was probably dumped and then I guess James was hijacked so he could carry out the next set of murders."

I turned to the monitor. Steve hadn't emerged from the storeroom. Unless he'd come out when I'd been looking at the photo, he and James were still in there. I picked up the walkie-talkie and pressed the talk button. "Steve, are you there?"

There was no answer other than crackling static.

"Maybe we should make sure they're okay," I said.

Felicity looked at the monitor, at the open door that Steve had gone through. That look of concern was still on her face. "Yes, we should."

We left the office and used the keycard to enter the inner part of the building, walking along the corridor in the direction Campbell had led us when James had locked himself in the storeroom. The swords in our hands cast an eerie blue glow over the walls.

When we got to the open storeroom door, I pushed my sword blade through the doorway to light the interior of the dark room. The enchanted glow picked out shelves and pieces of furniture covered in dust sheets but there was no sign of Steve or James.

I stepped inside and looked around. Felicity followed me and used her own sword's glow to illuminate the room.

"It's very dusty," she said, wrinkling her nose. "I can't see why James would bother stealing a key to come here."

"Probably because of that," I said, pointing my sword at a piece of furniture in the corner. The dust sheet that had covered it lay on the floor, revealing a decorative wooden frame carved in the shape of vines and ivy leaves.

The mirror from the crime-scene photo stood facing us, and pressed into the top-right corner of the glass was an old, dried, bloody handprint.

22

I heard a sound behind me and turned around, sword held ready to strike. The blade's glow illuminated Steve cowering in the corner. He was curled into a fetal position, knees up against his chest.

"It came out of there," he said, his eyes fixed fearfully on the glass. "It grabbed James and took him into the mirror. I froze. I'm sorry. I failed him."

I crouched next to him and put a hand on his shoulder. "Listen to me, Steve. You didn't fail anyone. You brought us here to help the patients and that's what we're going to do. When this is all done, and Butterfly Heights is rid of its problems, the patients will have you to thank."

He sat up, leaning heavily against the wall, and said through gritted teeth, "Unfortunately, I won't be here when that happens." A deep, red slash ran across his chest, pumping out blood at an alarming rate. "He got me," Steve said weakly. "He hit me with a hook."

"We need an ambulance," I said to Felicity. She already had her phone in hand and was dialing.

"No need for that," Steve said. "It's too late for me. Just promise me you'll get the damned thing." He laughed weakly. "I don't even know what it was."

"It was Mister Scary," I said. "And I will kill him."

"Thank you," he said quietly. His head fell to one side, his eyes staring unseeingly at the floor. The blood that had been pumping from the wound in his chest slowed to a trickle. I reached forward and closed his eyelids. He'd been a good man, concerned for the patients in this place. He didn't deserve to be taken by Mister Scary for no reason other than being in the wrong place at the wrong time.

I stood up and turned to the mirror. "I'm going through," I told Felicity. "Into the Shadow Land. Are you coming?"

She put her phone into her pocket and looked at me, her facial features highlighted by the blue glow from the enchanted swords. "Of course I'm damn well coming."

We stepped over to the mirror and I pushed the tip of my sword against the glass. It met no resistance and slid through, disappearing into the glass. "The portal is open," I said. "It's probably been open since

Fields activated it over seventy years ago. He's been using it to go back and forth ever since."

"Now we'll use it to get to him," Felicity said.

I nodded and stepped forward into the mirror. When I came out through the other side, I was in the same storeroom but now the walls were dark and seemed insubstantial, as if they were made of black smoke.

Felicity stepped out from the mirror and stood next to me. "So this is the shadow version of the hospital. It looks almost the same as the real version."

"But it isn't the same," I said. "There will be differences. Thoughts have power here and Mister Scary has had a long time to shape this version however he wants it. We have to be careful."

We left the room and stood in a dark, deserted corridor with closed doors running along the walls on both sides. Each door was numbered and bore a small hatch like the cells we'd seen in the basement.

I went over to the closest door and pulled back the hatch. Inside, a man lay curled up asleep on a bed. He was restless, as if having nightmares. Floating above the bed, a mass of black smoky tendrils writhed and twisted, occasionally reaching down and slithering over the man's sleeping form, making him stiffen and cry out in his sleep.

I stepped back from the hatch and Felicity looked into the cell. "Is that one of the patients at the hospital?"

"I don't know," I said. "Come on, we need to find James and Mister Scary."

We set off along the corridor, past the doors, to a shadow version of the day room we'd seen during our first visit to Butterfly Heights. Here, there were shadow people sitting at the tables, playing games with cards that were no more than squares of black smoke and chess pieces that were made of shadows.

"No sign of them here," Felicity said.

I stepped out of the room and back into the corridor. "I think they might be in the basement. That seems to be the center of activity in this place. It's where the Midnight Cabal was working on its project and it's where there's something locked away in a cell. It stands to reason that Mister Scary might run his own little project from there."

"That makes sense," Felicity said. "But how do we know where the basement is in this version of the hospital? Everything here is a bit different, including the floor plan."

I remembered how Leon and I had managed to escape the Shadow Land before, by thinking ourselves into the shadow version of Blackthorn House, where we knew there was a portal to the real world.

"You remember the basement door?" I asked Felicity.

She nodded. "Yes, of course."

"Close your eyes and think of it, imagine you're standing in front of it."

She looked at me incredulously but she said, "All right," and closed her eyes.

I did the same, picturing the basement door in my mind, the oaken wood and the brass plaque that said *Basement*.

When I opened my eyes, we were standing at the shadow version of the door. "Open your eyes," I told Felicity.

She opened them and they went wide when she saw the basement door. "How did that happen?"

"Like I said, thoughts have power here. I don't think the Shadow Land has a conventional geography. Its landscape is determined by mental images." I opened the door.

"And this version of the door is unlocked," Felicity said. "That's lucky, because we left the Janus statue in Steve's office."

"Even if it was locked, we could just think it unlocked. Maybe. There's a lot we don't know about this place."

"Well, let's find out what's in the basement," Felicity said.

We descended the spiral staircase, both of us on high alert in case Mister Scary should come rushing up at us.

When we reached the bottom, the shadow

version of the iron door was unlocked. I pushed the door open and we stepped through.

This version of the subterranean room wasn't like the one we'd seen in the real world. Where that room had been empty save for a desk and the Midnight Cabal logo on the wall, the shadow version was inhabited by shadow people.

Like the shadowy card and chess players we'd seen in the day room, the insubstantial people in this room seemed to be no more than a recording of what had once taken place here. They ignored us as we walked among them.

There was also shadow-furniture in the room; desks set against the walls and bookshelves along one wall. In the center of the room, a long table sat beneath a surgical light.

Some of the shadow people sat at the desks, writing in books, while others were gathered around the table, holding medical instruments. I walked over to the table to see what was lying on it.

The dark shape seemed to be a woman with wings. When I looked closer, I saw that she had the torso of a woman but the legs and feet of a bird. Her head was covered with some kind of hood.

"Felicity, any idea what this is?"

She came over and looked at the creature on the table. "Half-woman, half-bird. Probably a siren or a harpy. Oh, of course, it's a siren. The name Project Ligeia makes sense now. I thought it was named after the Poe story but Ligeia was also the name of one of the sirens in Greek mythology."

"Looks like the serum they were making was created from her blood," I said, watching the shadow doctors bending over the siren with their scalpels and needles.

Sadness filled Felicity's eyes. "Project Ligeia ended in 1942 when the Pinewood Asylum closed down. Do you think she's been locked in her cell all that time? For almost eighty years?"

"I think it's possible she's been a captive for much longer than that," I said. "When I had those visions earlier, I saw Midnight Cabal ships that looked like they were from the eighteenth century. I think the cabal members aboard those ships somehow captured her. She must have been moved to Pinewood Asylum in the late nineteenth century when it was built and was either forgotten or left to rot when the Cabal abandoned the place."

"That's awful. No creature should have to suffer like that."

"I guess that's why she's attacking the hospital staff and patients with her song. She's reaching out the only way she knows how. And what is Campbell's involvement in all of this? He knows about the siren in the basement and he had the project notebooks. Is he a member of the Midnight Cabal or did he stumble on the remains of their forgotten project and resurrect it for his own ends?"

Answers to those questions would have to wait. We still needed to find Mister Scary.

"We should check the cells," I said, indicating the door on the other side of the room. "Maybe Mister Scary has James locked up in there."

I opened the door that led to the cells and stepped through. The shadow version of this area of the basement was exactly the same as the real-world version: nine numbered cells with hatches on their doors.

We checked the eight cells situated on the sides of the corridor. They were all empty. That left the ninth cell, where we knew a siren was locked up in the real world.

I pulled back the hatch and looked inside.

The cell was much larger than the others and had a small circular pool at its center. The ceiling was at least fifty feet high and branches had been fixed to the walls at various heights. I assumed these were perches for the siren. The interior of the cell was like the inside of a giant birdcage.

A shadow version of the siren was huddled in the corner, wings drawn up around her body and overhead as she rocked slowly back and forth. Floating above her, a dark mass of tendrils writhed in the air, like the ones I'd seen over the patient's bed upstairs. Every couple of seconds, a tendril reached out and touched the siren's wings. She flinched and let out a low, mournful song that she seemed to be singing to comfort herself.

I stepped aside and Felicity peered through the hatch. "It looks like she's being tortured," she whispered. "Is Mister Scary doing this?"

"Either him or Campbell," I said. "I wouldn't put anything past the doctor at this point."

She closed the hatch. "So where is Mister Scary? He obviously isn't down here. And I can't think of any other parts of the hospital that would have a particular significance for him."

"Maybe he isn't in this building at all. There's a part of the Shadow Land where he builds the shadow houses, the part where Leon and I went. James said Mister Scary shows him things. Could he be showing him the murders he's committed, replayed over and over in those houses?"

"It's possible," Felicity said. "But how do we get there from here?"

"You remember what Blackthorn House looks like?"

"Yes, I think so."

"We can get there the same way we got to the basement door."

"All right. The image I remember best of Blackthorn House is from a photograph in the paper, taken from the garden."

"Yeah, me too."

She closed her eyes. I instinctively reached out

and took her hand. I wasn't exactly sure how this thought-travel worked and I didn't want to lose her in the Shadow Land.

I closed my own eyes and thought of Blackthorn House, the scene of the Bloody Summer Massacre, where Mister Scary had killed over a dozen high-school students and Mallory had been the only survivor.

When I opened my eyes again, I was standing on the lawn of Blackthorn House and Felicity was standing next to me.

She looked at the house and then at our surroundings. There were other shadow buildings here and Mister Scary had arranged them in two neat rows, forming a street. A street memorializing his kills.

"This is very macabre," she said.

"Yes, it is. If we can stop Mister Scary, he won't be able to add any more buildings to his collection. And the ones that are here will probably fade away over time, becoming nothing more than insubstantial smoke and memories."

"That's all the motivation I need," she said. "Let's kill the bastard."

We stepped up to the front door of Blackthorn House and opened it. As the door swung inward, we heard a scream from inside.

23

"That sounded like James," Felicity said, stepping into the house and checking the foyer around me. Something rushed at me from the darkness and I cried out in surprise, raising my sword in defense.

But it was nothing more than the shadow of a teenage girl, fleeing in terror from something unseen. I saw another fleeing shadow on the stairs, this one a young man desperately trying to get to the second floor, looking over his shoulder at an unseen assailant.

"This is the Bloody Summer Night Massacre," Felicity said. "Being replayed, just like you said."

"It wasn't like this when Leon and I were here, so Mister Scary must be able to replay that night at will."

"Which means he's here somewhere," she said.

"Yeah."

The scream came again, from somewhere on the

second floor. I ran up the stairs, sword ready, and burst into the first room I came to. There was nothing in here but a couple of dead shadow students lying on the floor, runes carved into their bodies.

There was a door to an adjoining room. I kicked it open and saw James Elliot, kneeling in the middle of a glowing magic circle on the floor. His head was bowed and he was shivering as if in pain.

"James," I said, rushing forward.

He stood up impossibly quickly, as if he were being dragged up by an invisible hand, and threw his head back, screaming again. Then he collapsed to the floor like a marionette whose strings had been cut. But where he had been standing, there now stood a dark figure made of black smoke, his skin alight with orange occult runes glowing all over his body. His eyes also glowed orange and, as the shadowy head turned to face me, they narrowed.

"Alec Harbinger," he said. His voice wasn't deep and threatening—as I'd always imagined it would be —but almost nonchalant. That worried me. He was confident enough in his abilities that he didn't feel the need to appear menacing.

"Mister Scary," I said. "Or do you prefer Henry Fields?"

"Henry Fields is no more. I shrugged off that burdensome jacket in 1942. I am beyond flesh."

"But you can't do your dirty work without it," I said, gesturing to James's prone body. I could see he was still breathing but judging by the way his chest rose and fell, the breaths were shallow.

"Some things require a physical body, true, but I am not trapped inside any single prison of flesh like you and the rest of your kind. I am free to roam at will, to do as I please."

"Not for much longer."

His dark face had no mouth but I was sure that if he had a mouth, he would be smiling at me patronizingly. "And who is going to stop me? You? Or your assistant over there?" He turned to face Felicity momentarily before fixing his orange eyes back on me. "Your swords are useless against me. I am eternal."

"Yeah, I don't think so."

The glowing eyes narrowed farther. "Eternal," he repeated.

"No, I don't buy it. If it were true, then why all the elaborate rituals when you go on your killing sprees? Why the runes carved into your victims' bodies? I never understood that until now. But now I can see those same runes on your body. You have to kill to stay alive—or whatever you call your sorry existence. You have to charge up those runes on your body by carving them into freshly-killed victims."

I took a step closer to him. "You may have traded in your old body but this new model requires maintenance, doesn't it? You need magical energy stolen from the bodies of dead teenagers, otherwise you'll wither and die like anybody else. So spare me your eternal bullshit."

He lunged at me, a shadowy hook suddenly appearing in his hand. I tossed up a magical shield and the hook dissipated against it. Mister Scary drew back, an identical weapon forming in his hand.

Felicity threw herself at him, her sword swinging at his head. The blade passed through his smoky body and Felicity was suddenly off-balance and crashing into the wall.

So, he hadn't been lying about the swords being useless against him. I summoned up my anger and directed it into my hand. Blue energy crackled around my hand in the form of magical symbols. I threw it at Mister Scary.

The energy bolt hit him in the chest and he doubled over as if in pain. I'd hoped to do more damage to him than that but at least now I knew he could be hurt by something. I summoned up another bolt.

Mister Scary decided to go for Felicity. I wasn't sure if he intended to kill her or take her hostage so I couldn't zap him again. I never got the chance to find out because Felicity rolled out of the way and Mister Scary caught nothing but air.

I threw a second bolt at him. The blue glowing projectile hit him in the face and the force of the impact sent him slamming into the wall.

"You okay?" I shouted to Felicity.

She was dragging James out of the circle toward the door we'd entered through. "I'm fine. Finish him."

I was about to tell her that I didn't think my magical bolts were having enough effect on Mister Scary to finish him when he suddenly pushed himself from the wall, hurling himself in my direction.

I saw the movement too late. Mister Scary lashed out with a shadow hook and I realized I didn't have time to put up a shield. Throwing myself backward, I tried to avoid the dark weapon but it slashed through the front of my shirt and I felt a stinging pain as it cut through my skin.

"Alec!" Felicity cried out, running over to me, waving her sword uselessly at Mister Scary.

He swung his hook at her, arcing it down toward her chest. Felicity's sword couldn't damage Mister Scary but when she raised the enchanted blade, it blocked his shadow weapon. The hook exploded into a thousand pieces of shadow.

She hadn't noticed a second hook in his other hand. He brought it up beneath her sword and I was sure it was going to slice her in half but she somehow managed to jump back. The shadow blade cut through her sweater and I heard her groan as it made contact with her flesh. I had no idea how deep it had gone but I knew we had to get out of here now. We weren't going to win this.

She was lying on her back, trying to get up. Mister Scary was looming over her, about to go in for the kill.

I conjured a shield and threw it up between him and Felicity. Then I dived over to where she was and took her hand. "Felicity, think of the storeroom. We need to get back to the storeroom." I discarded my sword and grabbed James's hand tightly. Then I closed my eyes and visualized the storeroom where we'd entered the Shadow Land through the old mirror.

When I opened my eyes, Felicity and I were in front of the mirror in the storeroom but James hadn't come with us. I'd been holding his hand but he'd been unconscious and hadn't visualized our destination. He was still in Blackthorn House with Mister Scary.

"Go through the mirror," I told Felicity. "I have to go back for James."

"I'm coming with you," she said. "I'm not too badly hurt."

I looked at her abdomen where Mister Scary's shadow hook had sliced through her sweater. A bright red line of blood stretched from below her navel all the way up to her sternum.

"It isn't very deep," she said. "I'm all right."

I checked my own wound, a similarly shallow cut that ran in a diagonal line across my chest. I'd have a scar but I'd live.

"Only my magic can hurt him," I told her.

"I'm not letting you go alone."

We didn't have time to argue and even if I went back to Blackthorn House without her, she could easily follow me. "Okay, let's go. There's a mirror portal in one of the bedrooms. Leon and I used it. We can drag James through there if he's still unconscious."

I closed my eyes and visualized the room where we'd fought Mister Scary. When I opened them, Felicity and I were in the room but it was empty. Mister Scary and James were gone.

"He didn't want to risk losing his newest body," Felicity said. "He could have taken James anywhere."

"We'll never find him." I picked up the sword I'd discarded and took a deep breath, trying to calm the emotions boiling inside me. We'd lost James and Steve to Mister Scary and there was nothing we could do about it. He'd won this round easily.

I vowed to myself that the next time we faced him, he would be destroyed. "We're going to need to find a way to kill him," I said.

"We'll find a way," Felicity said. "If it's the last thing we do, we'll find a way."

2 4

When we got back to Butterfly Heights—the *real* Butterfly Heights— I took an old blanket from one of the storeroom shelves and covered Steve's body with it. We were going to have to call the police later but right now, I needed to confront Dr. Campbell about Project Ligeia and find out if he was carrying on the work of the Midnight Cabal.

We got back to Steve's office and gathered up our things, putting the Cabal books into the backpack. "I guess we need to visit the doctor at his home," I told Felicity.

She nodded. "It shouldn't be too difficult to find his address."

But as we left the office and were walking toward the exit, Campbell entered the building, his face a mask of fury. "I should have known it was you," he said when he saw me. "Where's Steve? I need him to call the police. You've broken into my office and I'm going to press charges. You're going to jail, Harbinger."

"Really? You think if the police come here, it's me they'll be taking away in handcuffs?"

A confused look crossed his face. "Of course. For breaking and entering." He held up his phone. "My alarm went off and I got here to find you and your partner leaving the scene of the crime."

"I think they'll be more interested in what's been going on here. Your experiments. Project Ligeia. The siren in the basement."

The blood drained from his face. "What have you done to her? What have you done to Ligeia?" He sprinted for the door to the inner building. "This is why I told Steve no P.I.s. You kill what you don't understand." He went to put his keycard into the lock but looked suddenly fearful. He turned to face me and I saw apprehension etched into every part of his face. "Please tell me you haven't killed her."

"What's the deal, Campbell? What's really going on in this hospital?"

"Tell me you haven't killed Ligeia," he pleaded. Tears were streaming down his face now.

"I haven't killed her," I told him to put him out of his misery. "Yet. I want some answers right now. Tell me about Geraldine Hunsaker, Ryan Martin, and the serum that was being made from the siren's blood."

He put his back to the wall and slid down it,

either relieved that the siren was still alive or surrendering himself to the idea that his secret project wasn't so secret anymore. "I'll tell you everything," he said, "but you have to promise me you won't hurt Ligeia. None of this was her fault."

"Talk," I told him. "Let's start with the Midnight Cabal. Are you a member?"

He looked genuinely confused. "You mean they still exist? I found their books in the basement but I thought they were disbanded after most of their staff were killed in 1942."

"Okay, so tell me about the books. You read them and decided to continue Project Ligeia on your own?"

"Not at first," he said. "I read about the serum that could transform humans into faerie creatures. I even kept the box of syringes containing the serum. But I wasn't interested in attempting the metamorphosis until I found Ligeia locked up in her cell down there. She was beautiful. After seeing her, the serum suddenly became very important to me. If I could become like her, we could be together. She can't accept me as I am. She's been mistreated by humans for too long. I daren't even go into her cell. But if I became a faerie creature, we could leave here and start a new life together. So I injected myself with the serum."

I frowned at him, confused. "You look pretty human to me."

"It didn't work. I didn't know how long the transformation would take so I waited days, then weeks. It soon became obvious I wasn't going to transform. Then I read in the books that it only works on people who have some faerie blood in them already. The serum can amplify an already-existent faerie gene but it can't create one out of nothing." He sighed heavily. "I don't carry the gene."

"But Ryan Martin did," I said. "And Geraldine Hunsaker."

"I searched for people with the gene. It wasn't too difficult to find them because the gene also makes those people susceptible to visions, which means they usually end up at institutions like this one at some time or other during their lives. Hunsaker was the first gene-carrier I found. She came here for a while and I realized through her therapy sessions that she had faerie blood. I had to know if the serum worked but I couldn't risk injecting her at the hospital in case something went wrong. So I waited until she was discharged and traveled to her home. She was more than willing to let me inject her. As far as she was concerned, she was simply getting a house call from her doctor."

"So you changed her into a creature just to satisfy your own curiosity." I already disliked Campbell but this made me hate him. How could he toy with people's lives like that?

"It was glorious," he said, a smile flickering over

his lips at the memory. "I don't even know what it was that Geraldine became but she became half-snake, half-woman. She slithered away before I could stop her." He looked suddenly disappointed. "I don't know what happened to her."

"And then you did the same thing to Ryan Martin?"

"Yes, but this time, I gave him the injection here, believing he wouldn't be able to escape like Geraldine had. I was wrong about that. When the serum took effect, Ryan suddenly became paranoid and fled. You saw how he scaled the gate. I believe his transformation took place later, after he'd climbed into the storm drain."

He looked at me with pleading eyes. "My work isn't done. I know I can find a way to replicate the faerie gene and inject it into myself. Then I can use the serum to be with Ligeia. No one needs to know about this, Harbinger. You can let me go on with my work here. I'll pay you handsomely, of course."

"Not going to happen, Campbell. You've ruined lives, destroyed families, just so you can get your rocks off with a siren. It ends here."

The fear returned to his face. "What are you going to do?"

"First, I'm going to deal with the siren. Then I'm—"

"No!" He got up and swiped his keycard through

the lock. He ran through the door and pulled it closed behind him.

I got my own keycard out of my pocket and opened the door. Felicity and I ran along the corridor, trying to catch up with Campbell. His head start meant he reached the basement door long before we did and after he'd used his key to open it, he locked it behind him.

The Janus statue was in the backpack I was carrying but it was wrapped up and wouldn't open the basement door until it was unwrapped. I threw the backpack off my shoulder and opened it, unwrapping the statue as quickly as I could.

"Do you think he's going to open the siren's cell?" Felicity asked.

"Yeah, I do. He said he hadn't dared to go in there but now he has no choice. If he wants her to live, he's going to have to release her."

"And she's been locked up for decades, possibly hundreds of years. This isn't good, Alec."

"I know, so let's get down there as quick as we can." I pulled the cloth from the statue and the basement door clicked open. We ran down the steps, swords in our hands. That siren was going to be really pissed off when she finally got out of her cell.

I heard Campbell scream and increased my pace as much as I dared on the steep steps. When I got to the bottom, I rushed into the room with the Midnight

Cabal logo and over to the second door. "You ready?" I asked Felicity before I opened it.

"Ready," she said, brandishing her sword.

I opened the door, expecting a flutter of wings and a mass of striking claws.

But the corridor was quiet.

The siren's cell door was open and Campbell lay on the floor in a pool of blood. His body had been shredded by the same talons I'd been expecting to encounter. But the siren wasn't in attack mode, she was standing over Campbell solemnly, looking down at his dead body.

When she saw us, a resigned look spread over her face. As Campbell had said, she was beautiful but she also looked broken from her years in captivity. Her body was covered with scars. I wondered what tortures the Midnight Cabal had inflicted on her, what she had been forced to endure over hundreds of years.

Her dark eyes flickered to my sword and then she looked closely at me and nodded. She knelt down, folded her wings back, and stretched out her neck, inviting me to end her suffering.

I wasn't so sure I could do it. Had she actually done any wrong? She'd affected people in the hospital with her song but she hadn't actually killed anyone as far as I knew.

I lowered my sword. "I can't," I told her.

She sang a soft song and images filled my mind,

images of what she had endured at the hands of the Midnight Cabal from when she was captured in the 1700s to her time as a medical experiment here in this basement. "You can," she said.

I swung the sword and the enchanted blade cut cleanly through her neck, ending her suffering.

Felicity put her hand to her mouth and looked away but not before I'd seen the tears in her eyes.

25

We left the hospital and walked out into a night that was cold and wet. The rain was falling again, hissing down onto the lawn of Butterfly Heights.

When we were undercover of the trees, I fished my phone out of my pocket and called Bud Clarke, the head of the Salem branch of the Society of Shadows. I'd done Bud a favor a while back by dealing with a couple of demons that had killed a Massachusetts investigator. I was hoping he'd repay the favor tonight.

He sounded sleepy when he answered the phone. "Hey, Alec. What's up?"

"I need a cleanup," I told him. "Butterfly Heights Hospital, near Greenville, Maine. There's a dead siren in the basement and a couple of human casualties. Also, there are patients here that are going to need their usual care when they wake up in the morning, so a member of the medical team needs to be contacted."

"Consider it done. A siren, huh? I didn't know there were any of them still left in the world."

"Well, there's one less now."

"That's probably a good thing."

"Yeah, probably. Thanks, Bud." I ended the call.

"We should go and get those syringes from Campbell's house," I told Felicity.

"Yes, we should." She seemed distant.

"Everything okay?" I asked her when we reached the Land Rover.

"I'm just tired of seeing so much death," she said, climbing into the passenger seat. "And did the siren really have to die? It says in the Society of Shadows Investigative Handbook that a preternatural investigator can allow a preternatural being to live if he or she has determined that the creature has never harmed a human being."

"She killed Campbell."

"But he deserved it."

"Look," I said, starting the engine. "I didn't kill her because she killed Campbell. When she sang that song, she showed me the suffering she'd endured for hundreds of years. It was horrendous. She showed me those things so I'd understand why she wanted to be put out of her misery."

"Oh, I see. Then you did the right thing, I suppose."

"I did what she wanted. I don't feel great about it."

An hour later, we drove back to *Pine Hideaway*. A wooden box containing three filled syringes sat on the back seat of the Land Rover. Campbell's house had been easy enough to break into and the box had been sitting on the desk in his home office. We'd driven from his house to *Pine Hideaway* in silence, the only sound the patter of rain on the Land Rover and the metronomic whir of the wipers.

When we got inside the cabin, I lit a fire while Felicity sat on the sofa, her eyes unfocused.

"You sure you're okay?" I asked her as the fire began to crackle.

"Just exhausted," she said.

"Yeah, me too. We should probably take a shower before we hit the sack. Mister Scary shredded us up some."

She looked down at her torn sweater and the thin trail of dried blood that stretched across her abdomen. "I'd actually forgotten about that. Yes, I need to get cleaned up. And so do you." She stood up and walked to the foot of the stairs before turning to face me. "You did do the right thing, Alec. With the siren, I mean."

"Thanks."

She went upstairs and I heard the shower turn on, the water spraying into the tub for a few seconds before Felicity stepped in.

I sat on the sofa and turned my attention to the events of the night, closing my eyes and replaying them in my head, wondering if I should have done anything differently. I definitely needed to be more prepared before facing Mister Scary again and I made a mental note to research the runes I'd seen on his body. They might hold the key to defeating him.

I heard the shower go off and Felicity stepping out of the tub. The thought of climbing the stairs and taking a shower myself seemed like too much effort. I was too comfortable on the sofa in front of the fire.

The next thing I knew it was morning and my phone was ringing. I opened my eyes, confused by the morning light beyond the windows.

I grabbed my phone and checked the number. It was Joanna Martin. I hit the answer button. "Hi, Mrs. Martin."

There was a pause, during which I could hear her sobbing. Then, she said, "He's gone. Sammy's gone."

"What do you mean? Was he taken again?"

"No, I don't think so...I don't know. His backpack is missing, and some food from the refrigerator. I didn't even know he was gone until I woke up this morning. I don't know what to do. What should I do?"

"Have you called the police?"

"Yes, they're sending someone over here."

"We're on our way. Is there anywhere Sammy

might have gone? A friend's house maybe? Or somewhere he enjoys visiting, like a park?"

"He doesn't have any friends. And he barely goes beyond the yard."

"Okay, try to stay calm, we'll be there soon." I ended the call.

Felicity was halfway down the stairs, dressed in pink pajamas. "What's wrong?"

"Sammy's gone. It sounds like he ran away."

"Oh no, why would he do that?"

"I don't know but we need to get to Dearmont and help find him. The police may overlook certain aspects of his disappearance."

She ran back upstairs and into her room to get dressed.

I went up to the bathroom and took the quick shower I should have taken last night before quickly dressing and heading back downstairs. Felicity was already waiting by the door, her laptop and jacket under her arm. "Do you think Sammy left of his own accord?"

"I don't know," I said, grabbing my own jacket and opening the cabin door. "It seems strange that he'd run away from home a couple of days after he was abducted."

We went out to the Land Rover and got inside. The rain hammered on the roof and the dark clouds overhead meant it was dark enough to need the headlights. I turned them on, along with the heater.

Felicity shook rainwater from her hair. "This is terrible," she said.

Backing out onto the road, I said, "You mean Sammy disappearing again?"

She nodded and removed her glasses to wipe the rain from the lenses. "I mean this weather. That poor boy is outside in this terrible weather somewhere."

"He won't be outside," I said. "He has to take shelter or the daylight will hurt him." I just hoped that wherever he was, the daylight was the only threat to his safety.

26

When we got to the Martin residence, the rain had finally stopped and the dark clouds had parted to show a splash of blue sky. I parked at the back of the house as usual, behind a police cruiser, and Felicity and I went to the back door and knocked.

Amy Cantrell opened it. She glared at me and stepped aside to let us into the dark house. "Mrs. Martin told me she called you," she said. "I don't agree with her decision but I can't change her mind."

"Look, Amy, Victoria told me your dad's in some kind of enchanted sleep. I'm sorry. If I can do anything—"

"Save it. Unless you can help him, I'm not interested in anything you have to say. Can you help him? Because the witches sure can't."

I shook my head. "No, I don't think I can."

"Then let's get to the business at hand. Since Mrs. Martin wants you to be involved in the search for her son, I'll tell you what I know but it isn't much. It looks like the kid ran away during the night. Mrs. Martin checked on him at eleven, when she went to bed, and he was definitely in his room at that time. She says he was sitting at his desk, drawing. There isn't much else to tell. I have two teams of deputies and twenty volunteers searching Dearmont, the surrounding woods, and the lake. No one has found anything yet."

"Do you know how he left the house? Through the back door? Front door? A window?"

"He went out through the front door. It was unlocked when Mrs. Martin got up this morning."

That meant I couldn't use the faerie stones to track his movements. If Sammy had traveled along the streets, there wouldn't be enough trees around to show me the visions.

"Alec," Mrs. Martin said, appearing from the hallway, "thank God you're here. You found my boy before, you can do it again." Her eyes were red and she was clutching a balled-up tissue in her hand.

"I'll try," I told her. "Is there any reason why Sammy might have run away?"

"No," she said, wiping tears from her eyes. "I don't know why he'd do this. It isn't like him at all."

"Did you have an argument? Was he upset about anything?"

"No, he seemed just fine."

"And he was drawing when you last saw him in his room?"

She nodded. "Yes, he was sitting at his desk."

"Do you know what he was drawing?"

"No, I don't know."

"Is this really important, Harbinger?" Amy asked impatiently. "The kid is missing. Who cares what he was drawing?"

"Do you mind if I take a look?" I asked Mrs. Martin.

"No, of course not, if you think it will help. I'll go get it." She went back into the hallway and up the stairs.

Amy sighed. "I'm going to go help my team search the woods. This isn't getting us anywhere." She went out through the back door.

"I hope her father recovers soon," Felicity said, pulling aside the blinds and watching Amy leave. "It must be terrible for her."

"Yeah, maybe we should check in with the Blackwell sisters later and see how the sheriff is doing." I felt helpless because I couldn't do anything for the sheriff and also responsible, since it had been in my house that he'd come into contact with Excalibur.

Mrs. Martin came into the kitchen, a sheet of paper in her hand. She placed it on the kitchen table. "That's it," she said. "That's what he was drawing last night."

I looked at the picture. It was a drawing of Dearmont Lake and the spur of rock where I'd found the cave.

"I think I know where Sammy is," I said. "Mrs. Martin, come with us and we'll take you to him." The three of us went out to the Land Rover and Mrs. Martin climbed into the back seat.

As I backed out onto the road, I said, "I have something to tell you. You'll probably find it disturbing but I think it's best that I tell you the truth."

"Okay," she said, looking afraid of what I was about to tell her. She steeled herself for bad news. "Go ahead, I can take it."

I told her about Dr. Campbell and the serum. I left out the details regarding the Midnight Cabal but told her everything that pertained to her husband, including the fact that the serum had transformed him into the shellycoat that had taken Sammy.

When I finished, Mrs. Martin was in tears. "My poor Ryan," she sobbed. "How could this happen to him? What am I going to tell Sammy?"

"I think he may have already figured it out," I told her. "He has the second sight, after all, the same as you and your husband. I think that's why he's gone back to the place where the shellycoat took him."

She went quiet after that and I guessed she was

taking time to process the information she'd just been told. It was a lot to take in.

We arrived at the closest part of the highway to the rock spur, the place where Mrs. Martin had sped off in her Ford and left Felicity and me in the dust. I parked the Land Rover and we all got out.

I could already see a figure sitting on the rocky outcrop. "There's Sammy," I told Mrs. Martin.

"Sammy," she called, clambering over the rocks to get to her son. Felicity and I followed.

Sammy had dressed himself in long sleeves, gloves, jeans, boots, a scarf that he wore over his face and a pair of sunglasses. A wide-brimmed straw hat sat on his head. "Mom," he said. "I saw him again last night. He was out in the yard, under my bedroom window. I'm not scared of him anymore. We came down here together and I watched him swimming in the water over there. He's gone now, though." I couldn't see his face but I could hear disappointment in his voice.

I noticed that he was referring to the shellycoat as *him* now and not *it*.

Mrs. Martin came over and hugged me. "Thank you, Alec. Sammy and I believed Ryan was dead but you brought him back to us, no matter how changed he is. He's still my husband and Sammy's father. You hunted a monster but reunited a family. I don't know how I can ever repay you."

"There's no need," I said.

"Just let us know how you're doing from time to time," Felicity said. "Most of our cases don't have a happy ending so it's nice to have one that does."

Mrs. Martin grinned and nodded. "Yes, I'm sure we'll have a happy ending. I'll be sure to let you know."

"Do you want me to drive you and Sammy home?" I asked her.

"No, we'll stay by the lake a little while longer. Sammy obviously likes it here and it's good that he's out in the fresh air, even if he has to be cocooned in all that clothing."

"I'll tell the police to call off the search," I said. "Keep in touch. Bye, Sammy." I waved at him.

He waved back and said, "Bye, Mr. Harbinger and Miss Felicity."

We walked back to the Land Rover and I said to Felicity, "I really think this is one case that will turn out okay."

"I hope so. After the hideous events at Butterfly Heights, it's nice to have some good news for a change."

"There's just one thing missing, though," I said as I got behind the wheel.

"What's that?"

"Breakfast. We rushed all the way here from the lake and we haven't eaten yet."

"As your assistant, I'm sure I can arrange something. How does Darla's Diner sound?"

"Like music to my ears." I started the Land Rover. The engine purred to life.

27

A letter from Mrs. Martin arrived at *Harbinger P.I.* two days later. Felicity brought the small white envelope into my office and put it on my desk. I opened it and unfolded the two pieces of paper that were inside it. One was a drawing made by Sammy and the other was a handwritten note written by Mrs. Martin.

∾

Dear Alec and Felicity,

I hope you are both well and are taking a well-deserved break after working so hard on The Case of the Shellycoat. You asked me to let you know how Sammy and I are doing so I wrote you this letter. But as you read on, you'll realize that this is the only letter I will ever send to you.

After learning what happened to Ryan, I took a long hard look at the life Sammy and I lead. We are prisoners in this house with no money, no freedom, and not even any sunlight. For a long time now, we haven't been living at all but have only been existing.

Sammy understands that the shellycoat is his father. We had a long talk about it but I think he already knew anyway. He dreams things that his young mind might not be able to process otherwise. He dreamed that the shellycoat was Ryan.

Since the day we found Sammy at the lake, we have been going back there a lot, usually at night and visiting Ryan. Sammy said he would rather be a shellycoat than be trapped in a body that can't go out in the sun. I just want the three of us to be a family again.

So I have taken steps to ensure that both Sammy and I can get our wish. It isn't often in life that someone can have a wish come true. You provided the means for ours to become reality, even if you don't realize it yet.

I wish both of you all the best for the future. I will never forget you or what you have done for my family.

Best wishes

Joanna Martin

I handed the letter to Felicity and looked at the

drawing Sammy had made. When I saw what he'd drawn, I pushed my chair back and grabbed the Land Rover keys. Outside, I went to the rear of the building where the vehicle was parked and opened it, reaching for the box on the back seat. I opened it as Felicity caught up with me.

Inside the box, there was one syringe. The other two were missing.

"Well, she was sitting in there when you told her about Ryan and the serum," Felicity said. "She must have formulated her plan then, and ensured she could carry it out at a later date if she wanted to go through with it."

"She stole them," I said.

"There's still one left to send to the Society. At least the other two were put to good use."

"Don't tell me you approve of this."

She shrugged. "As I said before, it's nice to have a happy ending." She held up Sammy's picture. "So, are we going to put this on the office refrigerator?"

I looked at the drawing and let out a resigned sigh. It was like any family portrait a ten-year-old might draw except that instead of showing stick figures representing mom, dad, and the artist, it showed three shellycoats swimming in a lake.

2 8

Amy skidded to a halt outside the witches' house and rushed inside. Victoria had called her and told her to get here quick. Amy hadn't been doing anything other than sitting at her desk worrying about her dad so she'd jumped into her patrol car and put her foot down all the way here.

She was hoping against all hope that the Blackwell sisters were somehow mistaken and that her father was going to wake up exactly the same man he'd been before the ice had frozen him.

"Down here," Victoria called as Amy burst through the front door of the house.

Amy took the steps two at a time in her hurry to get to the basement. She was anxious to see her dad again but scared of what he might have become.

She entered the room with the runes on the walls and the cot in its center. The ice was totally gone. A shallow puddle of water on the floor was the only evidence it had ever existed at all.

Amy rushed toward the cot but the witches held her back. "We need to stay here," Victoria said. "At a safe distance."

The sheriff stirred slightly and then his eyes opened slowly.

"Dad," Amy said.

He sat up slowly and looked around the room. When he saw the three women, his eyes came to rest on Amy. "Amy," he said. "How are you?"

His voice wasn't altered in any way. She'd seen movies about people who were possessed and they always spoke in a sinister, deep growl. But her father was talking just like he always talked.

"Dad, is that you?"

He swung his feet over the edge of the bed and stood up slowly, stretching his back and neck and shoulders. "Sheriff Cantrell is in here," he said, still talking in his normal voice, "At least a part of him is. But I'll be using his body for a while."

Amy felt her heart drop. The witches had been right after all; there was another being inside her father.

"Let him go," she said. "Let my dad come back to me. All of him. Get out of his body."

"I can't do that just yet so you might as well work with me rather than against me. I need the answers to a couple of questions, the most important being where is the sword-wielder?"

"What?"

"Alec Harbinger. Where is he?"

"I have no idea. Probably at his office."

"My other question is this: has he used Excalibur yet?"

"How should I know?"

He looked from one witch to the other. "Do either of you know?"

"No," Victoria said.

"Why are you so interested in Alec Harbinger?" Amy asked.

Her dad finished stretching and walked toward the door. "Because he is the sword-wielder and I am the sword's guardian. I'm here to make sure he doesn't screw up."

He began ascending the steps.

"Wait, Dad."

He stopped and looked down at her from the steps. "As I told you, your father is in here but I am not him. You should probably address me by my own name."

She was starting to get pissed off with his attitude. "Oh really? And what's that?"

He smiled thinly. "I have a number of names but you can address by the one you have probably heard before." He performed a short bow and said, "My name is Merlin."

COMING SOON!

USEFUL LINKS

Society of Shadows - Harbinger P.I. Reader Group on Facebook: https://www.facebook.com/groups/383500412074735/

Harbinger P.I. Mailing List (receive news of upcoming books): http://eepurl.com/bRehez

To contact the author:
adamjwright.author@gmail.com

CPSIA information can be obtained
at www.ICGtesting.com
Printed in the USA
BVHW031323180920
589140BV00001B/14